THEIR BORDER DESTINY

Men of the Border Lands 11

Marla Monroe

MENAGE EVERLASTING

Siren Publishing, Inc.
www.SirenPublishing.com

A SIREN PUBLISHING BOOK
IMPRINT: Ménage Everlasting

THEIR BORDER LANDS DESTINY
Copyright © 2014 by Marla Monroe

ISBN: 978-1-62741-120-2

First Printing: April 2014

Cover design by Les Byerley
All art and logo copyright © 2014 by Siren Publishing, Inc.

Printed in the U.S.A.

PUBLISHER
Siren Publishing, Inc.
www.SirenPublishing.com

THEIR BORDER LANDS DESTINY

Men of the Border Lands 11

MARLA MONROE
Copyright © 2014

Chapter One

Hunger gnawed at her stomach like an angry dog. Destiny Fields couldn't remember the last time she'd had a decent meal. For most of the last six months, she'd managed on next to nothing as she slowly made her way west, hoping to locate her cousins, who she thought lived in the Montana area. She had nowhere to go and no one else to turn to.

"We're stopping here for the night, guys. Let's get camp set up before it gets dark." Bill, the owner of the supply bus heading for Barter Town, set the parking brake and climbed out of the bus.

Destiny didn't say a word as she and the other man riding with them began pulling out the cook stove and stacking boxes to make room for them to bed down for the night. It wasn't safe to sleep out in the open. Not only were there all sorts of desperate outlaws waiting to get the drop on you, but the wolves and other wild animals in the area would tear them up given half a chance.

"You still branching off on your own?" Bill asked as he opened a can of beans and poured it into the boiler on the camp stove.

"Yep," she said in a low voice.

It wasn't safe for a woman to travel alone, so she was pretending to be a young teenage boy. There were very few women left in the US since the year of catastrophes had killed so many. The plagues and fevers that followed thinned out even more of the survivors. Some ten years earlier, tornadoes, floods, earthquakes, and tsunamis had wiped out whole cities. As far as she knew, it had happened all over the world. Now people lived the best way they could, with many becoming scavengers just to survive.

She'd been living with her aunt and uncle in old Atlanta ever since she'd lost her parents. Then a fire killed them, destroying their home and leaving Destiny all alone in the world. While living with them, she'd remained in the house, never leaving for fear that someone would take her. She was a young woman, making her a priceless commodity in the new world.

"Gonna be awful hard to live out there all alone," he said.

"Got family not far away from here. I'll be fine." She kept her head down, trying to will her stomach not to growl.

"I could use your help in Barter Town. You might find work there afterwards as well." Bill seemed to be trying awfully hard to get her to stay. It made her uneasy.

"Thanks, but they'll be watching for me. I need to head out first thing in the morning."

Bill didn't say anything more. He stirred the beans and turned to the other man to talk. Destiny ignored them and tried to figure out what she was going to do next. There was no way she was going into Barter Town. She'd heard too many horror stories about the place. Women were chained in brothels and sold like cattle. Fighting was a sport there, and no one was safe. There was no way she would survive in a place like that.

Twenty minutes later, Bill ladled a spoonful of beans onto her plate along with a hunk of dried-out bread. She tried not to devour it in one bite, knowing it could be the last thing she had to eat for a while. When she'd finished eating, Destiny wiped out her plate and helped Bill clean up. They bedded down in the bus, the door bolted closed and the windows shut tight. It was stuffy and warm inside, but it was too dangerous to leave even a crack in the windows that someone could use to get inside.

At twenty-two, Destiny felt years older. It seemed as if she'd spent her entire life hiding, first with her aunt and uncle, never going outside for fear of being stolen, and now, as a teenage boy making his way to family out west. She prayed she found them before she either died of starvation or was found out and taken. The acidic taste of fear made her stomach heave, threatening to reject the meager meal from earlier. She fought back the nausea and tried to make her body relax, one muscle at a time.

She had no idea what was ahead of her, but she prayed she would find a safe place to stay soon. She was exhausted and so hungry. Her breasts ached from being wrapped so tightly to keep anyone from guessing she wasn't a boy. Nothing had prepared her for living like this. She'd thought having to live her life inside her aunt and uncle's house for the last few years was bad enough, but this was far worse.

Being alone with no one to trust kept her nerves on edge. She had to watch her voice, keeping it as low as possible, and she had to watch her temper as well. She couldn't afford to piss someone off. Destiny had no doubts she'd get her ass beaten and run the risk of them discovering she was actually a woman. That would be very, very bad.

Because she was always on guard and didn't trust anyone, she rarely slept well. It seemed like every creak of the bus or a howl of a wolf or coyote would jar her awake. Tonight was no different since she knew come morning she would be striking out on her own once again. Even though she didn't trust Bill or the other man, she felt safer being with them than alone in a place she'd never been before.

Get some sleep, idiot. I'm not going to be able to walk far if I'm exhausted. Stop worrying about tomorrow. Nothing I can do about it tonight except try and rest up for it.

Destiny turned over and finally fell asleep.

* * * *

"Hell!" Marty Oleander pulled off the side of the road despite the fact that there were few vehicles on the road anymore. "How in the hell did I pick up something to give me a flat tire?"

Jumping out of the truck's cab, he walked around to the passenger side of the truck and, sure enough, the back tire was flat as a pancake. One more thing to have to look for in the next town he found. He rummaged around in the back of the truck and located the jack and a wrench. After loosening the lug nuts, he pulled the spare tire from beneath the truck's bed and then proceeded to change the tire.

Twenty minutes later, he returned everything, but didn't bother wasting space in the back with the blow tire. It couldn't be repaired anyway. He left it well off the side of the road and climbed back in the truck. Leaning his head back against the back of the seat, Marty rested a few precious minutes, sipping occasionally from a bottle of water. He felt as if he'd been on the road for months now.

When all hell broke loose almost seven years ago, he'd been a rookie police officer right out of the academy. Less than eight months on the job out of a house in south Chicago, and Marty learned what true anarchy looked like. For the next two years he had tried to continue working to keep innocents safe in the new chaotic state they lived in.

Wave after wave of disasters, including the aftermath of diseases that swept through the city, left people scared and desperate. You became a predator, or you were the prey. Many of his fellow cops had disappeared from one day to the next. Some had just stopped coming to work, choosing instead to protect and take care of their families, while others were never heard from again. Marty figured some had fled the city's inner turmoil and hostility, but some had probably been killed. Wearing a uniform, now more than ever, made you a target.

As time passed, even his superiors became corrupt, taking bribes in the form of food and supplies to line their store rooms. He kept trying to do the right thing, but when the same man he'd protected with his life only months before tried to kill him one day, Marty gave up, losing his faith in humanity. In his eyes, there was no such thing as innately good anymore. Man was out for what he could get, and to hell with whoever was in his way.

Marty had no close relatives still living. His sister and her family lived in Arizona, if they were even still alive. He hadn't heard from her since before the disasters had wiped out most forms of communication across the nation. His parents had died in an accident a year before everything went crazy. He'd been dating a nice woman at the time, but when he'd gone looking for her, he couldn't find her. No one seemed to know what had happened to her. He had no idea if she was still alive somewhere or not.

He had drifted around doing odd jobs to keep food in his belly for a year until he couldn't take the constant sounds of agony and despondence that never seemed to go away. Now he was heading in the general direction of Montana where he'd heard there were communes of families living off the land there. He hoped he would find peace out there. As it was, he had nothing to lose. Staying in Chicago wasn't an option anymore. He was slowly going crazy. The screams of women being raped and children going hungry were too much to take.

Marty stretched and started the truck once again. He needed to find shelter for the night. It would be dark soon. He'd slept in his truck a few times, but he didn't like doing it. Not only was it as uncomfortable as hell, it wasn't safe. He liked to find an old house or store that had been abandoned so that he could barricade the entrances from the inside.

As he pulled back onto the road, it occurred to him that he'd turned twenty-nine a few days past and hadn't even thought about it until then. He chuckled to himself. At twenty-nine, he'd thought he would be married with at least one kid by now. His older sister had three. At least she'd had three when he'd last spoken to her. Now he didn't even know if she or any of her family was still alive.

"No use dwelling on something I can't do anything about. Concentrate on staying on the road and finding shelter, Marty." He gripped the steering wheel with both hands, reminding himself not to go above sixty. It was the best speed to conserve gas and still get somewhere before full dark.

Three hours later, he pulled up next to what had once been a country bar and grill, according to the sign out front. He didn't see any signs of life, but he carried his weapon with him as he checked it out. He had about an hour until sunset and needed to secure the building if he was going to stay there. As much as he would rather have found an old house, the few he'd passed had looked occupied. This was the first building that looked in decent shape and empty since he'd had the flat tire.

He disturbed an armadillo and a nest of rats, but there was no sign of humans or wolves using the place. Marty quickly settled on the storage room as the best place to bed down for the night since there were no windows and the door actually had a deadbolt on the inside. He couldn't imagine why that was, but he was thankful all the same.

After unloading everything of value into the small space, Marty quickly explored the kitchen and found a few cans of vegetables along with a sack of dried beans. He added them to his stash, laid out his bed, and locked himself inside. When he turned off the lantern, the room plunged into darkness. Every noise in the building seemed magnified with the dark enveloping him. Having lived in Chicago all of his life, Marty still couldn't get used to the complete darkness of his new world. When the sun set back home now, there was no electricity to illuminate the night. Still, locked down inside a small room without windows was the ultimate in being in the dark. He didn't like it. Not one damn bit.

Chapter Two

Destiny was grateful for the new hiking boots she'd gotten back in Atlanta before starting on her trip to find her cousins. The first few weeks had been tough, but now they were well broken in and helped keep her from breaking her ankles negotiating the uneven terrain she had found herself on.

The paved roads would have been much easier to travel, but they also offered the most chance of being attacked. She used an expensive compass and maps to stay on track. While she'd been sequestered in her aunt and uncle's home for all of those years, she'd spent her time reading and learning everything on survival that she could. Her uncle brought home books from the library every time he ventured out to work or find food, leaving her and her elderly aunt at home.

Even though she'd never actually been camping in her life, Destiny had tons of knowledge catalogued in her brain, finding that she could figure it all out as she went along. She avoided the larger towns and cities where crime ruled. Instead, she kept mostly to herself, only venturing to the smaller towns when she needed supplies she couldn't scavenge or to work for a place to sleep. Today was one of those times she needed to find somewhere to hole up for a few days, so she could rest and regain some of her strength. The last week had been hard on her after leaving the supply bus to continue on her own.

She'd been heading roughly northwest and hadn't located a single place that looked safe enough to use as shelter for more than a night. She could tell the weather was about to change, and she didn't want to be caught out in a storm. More than likely it would cool off some with the rain, which sounded good in theory, but trying to walk through wet vegetation with cooler temperatures was just asking for pneumonia. That was a death sentence for sure.

Destiny studied the map once again and made some calculations. She should be close to where a community had once lived by now. Soon she should start seeing homes that would be scattered out around a small town. God let her not have made a miscalculation somewhere along the way. She was so tired and hungry.

After putting everything away, she stood up and started walking once again. Each step she took seemed to be more and more difficult. She realized after about thirty minutes that she was on the verge of exhaustion. If she didn't stop soon and rest for more than fifteen or twenty minutes, Destiny wasn't sure she would be able to recover enough to make it at all. The idea of bedding down out in the open terrified her. She was sure something terrible would happen to her if she did. No, it was better to keep going until she found somewhere relatively safe.

An hour later, the sound of voices had her stopping to listen. It took her a few seconds to calm her racing heart so she could hear better.

"Need someone to help us with this blasted garden, Dave. I'm tired of working sun up to sundown all the time," one man said.

"Harper, you rarely work a good eight hours as it is. I don't know what you're complaining about," another man said.

"If Jason would let the women out of the house to help us it wouldn't be so bad. I mean, at least it would be someone helping, and we'd have a pretty woman to look at while we worked," the first man spoke again.

"Well, that ain't happening. He's too scared something will happen to them. He's probably right, you know. Between the damn wolves and bears and those black market agents roaming around, a woman ain't safe out in the open."

Destiny listened for a few more minutes, then slowly backed away from them so they couldn't hear her as she walked around them. She wasn't thrilled with their conversation, but it sounded like they wouldn't turn down some help in exchange for food and a place to sleep. She didn't have a lot of options at the moment. Provided they didn't find out she was a woman and not the teenage boy she was pretending to be, Destiny felt like it was the perfect place to rest for a few days.

She quickly located the drive leading up to a two-story house with a very large garden stretched out behind the house and woods on either side. She approached the front porch in a slow stride with her hands out by her sides. She was sure someone would see her before she made it to the porch, and she didn't want them to shoot first and ask questions later.

Sure enough, a tall man stepped out on the porch with a rifle cradled in his arms. He looked very comfortable with it to her. She stopped walking and stared out from under her hat, forcing a smile to her face.

"Hi there. I was wondering if you had some work I could do for a place to sleep and some food for a few days. I'm making my way out to my cousins' place on the other side of Montana." Destiny held her breath in hopes the man wouldn't just chase her off his property.

"You don't look like you can do much work. You're a scrawny thing. How old are you?" the man asked.

"I'm nineteen, and I'm stronger than I look," she answered, keeping her voice pitched low.

He grunted and motioned for her to come closer. Destiny had to make her feet move toward the porch and the man who could either shoot her, send her on her way, or offer her a place to rest and food in her tummy. Her gut feeling was that it wasn't the best of choices, but since she really didn't have anything else to choose from, she needed him to agree to let her work for food and a place to rest.

After staring her over for a full minute, the man nodded. "Come with me."

Destiny followed him around to the back of the house where a barn stood not far from the garden. He opened the door and led her inside. Inside were three horses and a great deal of farming equipment. The place was in decent shape, but it needed work. The smell of grass and manure was strong but comforting in a way.

"Here you go. You can bunk down here at night." He indicated an empty stall. "Stow your things here, and I'll show you what needs doing in the garden. Won't be long 'til it's time to pull it all up and till it under for the winter."

He didn't give her much time to pull off her pack and drop everything to the floor before he was striding across the barn once again. Destiny followed him back out to a small shed he opened up.

"Here are the garden tools. Keep them clean and straight. You can start by gathering anything that looks ripe and carrying it to the back door. Just knock and leave the basket on the steps. Someone will come out and get it. Then start hoeing the weeds that are trying to take over. Dinner will be around dark. Wash up and knock on the back door. Someone will hand you out a plate. Any questions?" he asked.

"Uh, no, sir. I'll get to work now." Destiny swallowed at the amount of work to be done.

The garden was almost as large as a football field. But then, considering that there were at least five other people, if not more, living there, they would need a large garden to feed themselves.

She selected a basket and hurried back to the garden to start gathering anything that was ripe. She prayed she chose the right ones, and soon she filled the basket with everything from tomatoes, to beans, to cucumbers. When she filled one basket all the way up, she placed it on the steps and knocked on the back door before returning to the shed to locate another basket. By the time she'd filled that one and left it at the back door, Destiny was already exhausted. Where she was going to get the energy to hoe, she didn't know.

She took a quick break and drank some water from the water hose. After wiping sweat from her face, she glanced at the sky and noted that clouds were building. It would probably rain that night, but it wasn't the storm she was expecting. No, this one would just be a small squall compared to one that was building up. She wasn't sure how she knew, but she'd always known when the weather would turn ugly. Didn't matter if it was going to snow or rain, she just knew when and if it was going to be bad.

Taking the hoe out into the garden, she located the worst areas of grass and started there. It was hard work. She wished she had gloves, but she hadn't seen any in the shed. She would remember to get some the next time she ventured into a large enough town with an abandoned store she could look through. Gloves would always come in handy.

Two hours later, she stopped and sat down where she was to rest. Sweat poured off of her, and she was shaky all over. After she had rested for a few minutes, Destiny climbed back to her feet and carried the hoe back to the shed. She made sure it was clean and dry, then washed up as well. It was nearly dark now, and she was starving to the point that her belly hurt more than ached.

She knocked on the back door and waited for someone to bring her something to eat. After what seemed like forever, a man stepped out and handed her a plastic bowl with beans and a hunk of bread. While it was more than what she'd gotten when working on the supply bus, it still wasn't much. She took it from the man without saying anything. He glared at her before turning around and walking back inside the house, slamming the door behind him.

Once she'd finished eating, she rinsed out the bowl and left it on the back steps. Her weary legs barely carried her back to the stall in the barn. She rolled out her bed and curled up under the thin blanket. It wasn't long until she heard rain against the metal roof of the barn. It lulled her gently into sleep.

* * * *

Granger McCall watched the goings on around the house he'd found that morning. He normally didn't approach a place until he had thoroughly staked it out for long enough he knew what to expect if he did decide to ask for work. This one wasn't the type of homestead he really wanted to stop at, but he was low on supplies and the last three days it had rained a cold drizzle that spoke of the colder weather to come. He needed to rest then get back on the road. He wanted to find a nice, dry place close to a settlement where he could barter for food while staying warm during the winter months.

He counted a total of four men, two women, and one teenage boy. The boy was scrawny, but he seemed to be doing most of the work in the garden. One of the men stayed in, or close to, the house at all times while the other two disappeared into the woods. He figured they were going hunting. Now was as good a time as any. He hated dealing with people, but he had no choice if he was going to get a place to stay for a few days.

Granger slowly walked up the drive, stopping when the man who had stayed inside walked out on the porch with a rifle in his hands.

"What do you want?" the stranger asked.

"Looking for a place to rest for a few days. Been on the road a long time. I can chop wood for you. Get you a good stack for winter," he said.

"You look strong enough. Each day you stack a cord up for me, I'll let you stay in the barn and feed you two meals a day." The other man looked at him like he figured Granger would shake his head and leave.

"Sounds fair to me. I'll stow my stuff in the barn. Where's your ax, and I'll get started."

The other man hesitated then nodded. "It's out in the shed, next to the garden. Got a boy working the garden out there. Don't scare him off."

Granger just grunted and headed toward the barn. He located an empty stall that happened to be next to the one the boy looked to be using. He stared at the boy's stuff but didn't rummage through it. He didn't nose around other people's property. Just because he didn't trust anyone didn't mean he was going to act untrustworthy.

When he walked up to the shed, the teenager emerged from the garden carrying a hoe. He looked like he was barely standing on his feet. When he caught sight of Granger, he stopped, much like a deer froze when it heard something. The boy's eyes were a pretty shade of hazel with more green than brown in them. His face seemed feminine and slim for a boy, but then everything about the boy was small. He couldn't have been much more than five foot four or five with a thin build and graceful appearance. His chin-length brown hair had obviously been cut by his own hand and looked ragged even to him.

"I'm working for a few days for a place to sleep. Won't be bothering you," he told the boy. "Just getting the ax to cut fire wood."

Granger continued to the shed and located the ax. He checked the sharpness and was pleased to see it was sharp. He closed the shed back and nodded once again to the boy who still hadn't moved a muscle before walking back to the stump they used for cutting wood. It was obvious that was what it was used for by the wood chips and splinters of log on the ground around it. Someone didn't know the first thing about cutting wood. That was obvious.

In no time he had worked up a sweat and gotten into the rhythm of swing, split, stack, and set up. Over and over, he swung the ax, creating perfectly split firewood that would burn well. More than likely what they had been using was so poorly cut that it either burned too fast or was difficult to get started. Most people didn't know that how you cut wood affected how it burned.

Once he had a little more than a cord split and stacked, Granger cleaned the ax and replaced it in the shed. Then he cleaned up the area around the stump where he'd been working. He didn't like cutting wood with a mess on the ground around him. If he stepped on something and lost his balance, he could end up cutting himself on the ax.

After cleaning up, he watched the teenage boy clean the hoe then wash up as well. He followed him to the back door where the kid knocked then stood back and waited. Finally, one of the men he'd seen earlier walked out with two bowls in his hands. He handed one to the boy and the other to Granger. It was obvious by the expression on the man's face that he didn't like Granger one bit. Well, that was fine by him. He wasn't trying to win any popularity contest. He just wanted some food in his belly and a roof over his head for a few days.

When they sat down to eat, he noticed the kid didn't have as much as he did. Then again, he didn't have all that much himself. Still, he had the overwhelming urge to offer the kid some of his. Instead, he carried his bowl over to the stump and used it as a seat to eat. The kid just sat on the steps where he was. Granger dug in, and, when he looked up again, the boy was nowhere to be seen.

After he'd rinsed out his bowl and set it next to the one the boy had left on the steps, Granger returned to the barn to get some sleep. When he passed the stall next to his, he could hear the faintest of noises coming from the other side of the door. It would be easy to look over the top and see what the boy was doing, but Granger didn't much care what the sound was from. He walked into his area and closed the door. Then he spread out his bedding and lay back.

The bastards weren't feeding them much considering the work they were doing. He could always supplement what he got with some of the jerky he still had left from trading a deer he'd killed a while back. He doubted the boy had anything to fall back on. Something about the teenager called to him. He'd never been one to care about what happened to others before. Well, not since he'd gotten out of prison about three years before everything had gone to hell.

In another lifetime, Granger had been an upstanding citizen working as an accountant for a firm that audited hospitals. He had a nice condo in Pittsburg, a fiancée, good friends who he hung out with regularly, and he was about to get married. He'd had it made, or so he thought. Then one day everything fell apart. His best friend Eric and his fiancé had set him up to take the fall for Eric's scheme to filter millions of dollars from their clients over nearly a year. He'd never seen it coming.

It had all been a set up from the beginning. It had been Eric who'd introduced him to Laura in the first place. They'd hit it off instantly. Now Granger knew it was only because Eric had fed her everything that he'd liked in a woman, making her pretty much irresistible to him. She'd seemed perfect to him, and it wasn't long before they were living together. All that time, his best friend was screwing her behind his back and setting him up to go to prison.

Together, Laura and Eric had gotten away with well over ten million dollars, and Granger had taken the fall for something he hadn't done. It didn't matter that they never found the money. All that mattered was that it was his codes used to access accounts and his passwords used to get into the system after hours. Why no one had caught on to it sooner, Granger didn't have a clue. It wasn't until much later that he realized what had happened. Still, no one would believe him, and with nothing to his name, he only had a public defender who didn't give a rat's ass about him or his claims.

He'd been reading an old newspaper and saw where Eric, his supposed best friend, and Laura, his ex-fiancé, had gotten married and were honeymooning for two weeks in Cancun barely a month after he'd been convicted. Neither Eric nor Laura had enough money between them to afford a honeymoon in Cancun, much less two weeks.

He'd spent six years of his life inside those walls and only gotten paroled so early because he wasn't a violent offender and they were overcrowded. He'd kept to himself and avoided trouble as much as possible, but trouble had a way of finding you when you were inside. He had the scars to prove it. One of them he saw any time he looked in a mirror. It reminded him that people weren't to be trusted. Man was inherently untrustworthy as far as he was concerned. No one really cared about anyone other than themselves.

When the catastrophes started, his theory on man's descent into madness began to manifest in the world around him. Entire cities were destroyed in earthquakes, fires, and tornadoes. The tsunami that took out most of southern California left behind a vast wasteland and no survivors. In the aftermath of everything, he watched as people turned into thieves, murders, and scavengers with little regard for anyone but themselves. His faith in humanity had been totally destroyed, and now the tiny flame of hope that one day he'd be proved wrong had been destroyed.

As soon as it became obvious that there would be no overseeing anyone's parole anymore, Granger gathered supplies and headed west. The east coast was a complete mess, with the infrastructure in total meltdown. Where the West, he heard, had been devastated by tornadoes and fires, there wasn't as much disease there like there had been in the larger cities.

Granger had no desire to settle down anywhere, but after years of wandering from place to place, he realized it was time to settle down and carve out a safe place for himself. More and more people were heading west to escape the turmoil in the cities. He stood a much better chance of being left alone if he went toward the northwest part of the states where few people wanted to live with the intensity of the winters. That suited him fine. Let them repopulate the center of the country if they could. He'd live out his days without having to worry about anyone else screwing him over.

He lay there thinking about what all he needed to do once he found a place to stay. It occurred to him that he hadn't heard any noise from the stall next to him lately. The kid must have fallen asleep. Despite the fact that he shouldn't care one way or another, Granger couldn't help but wonder what he was doing at his age, living in the wilds all alone. It couldn't be easy on him. His size and the dark circles under his eyes attested to that. Something about the boy made

Granger want to hold him. He wasn't normally attracted to men, but for some reason, he was to this kid. Kid was the right word, too. He couldn't be much over seventeen or eighteen, much too young. Thoroughly disgusted with himself, Granger rolled over and went to sleep.

Chapter Three

The weather grew cooler, and Granger found himself helping the kid clear the garden one day. It had been a week, and he was about ready to move on again. They were barely feeding them enough to keep them alive to work for them, so it wasn't worth it to Granger to remain any longer. Oddly enough, the only reason he'd stuck around as long as he had was because of the kid. He hated to leave him for some reason. They barely said two words to each other all day, but he was reluctant to leave.

Granger worked in the back half of the garden while the teenager worked the top half. He'd noticed the kid had looked worse than usual that morning when they'd eaten the meager hash they'd been given. Still, he hadn't said anything and went about his work without complaint. He'd just about decided to ask the kid to stick with him when he left. More than likely he'd regret it down the line, but he couldn't leave him here. He'd talk to him tonight after dinner.

He heard yelling and cursing coming from the front section of the garden. Granger didn't think, he just ran in that direction. He had a bad feeling that something was happening to the kid. When he almost ran over them, Granger stopped and grabbed one of the men beating the kid.

"What in the hell are you doing? He's just a kid, and there are four of you," he yelled.

"He was stealing food," the man said, jerking his arm out of Granger's grip.

"Just a rotten tomato. That's all." The kid tried to cover his head and face as the men hit and kicked him.

Granger wasn't about to stand by and let them kill the kid for eating a rotten tomato. They didn't near 'bout feed them enough as it was. He roared and started pulling them off the boy, making sure they wouldn't take another shot at him in the process. When all four of the men were on the ground holding their stomachs or faces, Granger helped the kid up.

"I think you've done enough damage for one rotten piece of food," he said as he helped the boy back to the barn.

"T–thank you. They'll make you leave now," the boy said in a low scratchy voice.

"I was getting ready to leave anyway. They don't feed us enough for the work we do. Why don't you leave in the morning with me?" he asked.

"I'll think about it. Thanks." The boy rolled over to his side and curled up in a ball.

The sight of it tore at something inside of him. He wanted to wrap his arms around him and keep him safe. It didn't make sense. He'd never had feelings for another man before. He didn't have anything against two men being together. It just wasn't his preferences. Or at least it never had been in the past. Shaking his head, Granger closed the stall door and walked over to his.

There was no doubt they wouldn't feed them tonight. He chewed on some jerky, planning to offer some to the boy in the morning. They'd get up before dawn and leave, safer that way. Leaving before dark wasn't a good idea, or he would have left immediately. Instead, he settled down and closed his eyes.

Early the next morning, before the sun had even risen, Granger quietly gathered his things then opened the stall door next to his to wake the kid up. To his surprise, it was empty. The kid had picked up his things and left sometime in the night. He crouched down and felt the area where the boy had been sleeping and found it cold to the touch. He'd been gone for at least an hour. He prayed the kid was okay. He'd been pretty badly beaten before he'd gotten there to stop it.

Granger sighed and pulled on his pack. He walked out of the barn and headed down the road. He knew the general direction he planned to take, so he didn't bother reviewing his maps right away. Instead, he let his mind wander as he walked. Around ten, he stopped in a clearing to eat and rest. He opened a can of beef stew he'd been saving and ate it slowly, relishing the taste after the diet of beans, watery hash, and stale bread he'd had for the last week.

After cleaning up, he stood to start walking again when he heard the sound of a truck. By the time he'd made it to the main road, the truck had caught up with him. To his surprise, the four men from the house jumped out and surrounded him.

"What's going on?" he asked, dropping his pack and keeping his hands relaxed out by his sides.

"A little payback. You got the drop on us yesterday, but that ain't happening today," one of the men said.

"You were beating a defenseless boy for no reason," he said in a calm voice.

"The bastard stole from us. That's reason enough," another of the men said.

"That's bullshit," he said.

They didn't say anything else. Instead, they all rushed him at once. He got in some good shots, but with that many, he didn't stand a chance. They had him tied to a tree and helpless to stop them from beating him to death in less than two minutes. He had no doubt they didn't intend for him to walk away. He snorted. No good deed ever goes unpunished.

"Don't think you have anything to be laughing about, big man," the first guy said with a sneer.

"Where did you get that scar on your face anyway?" another of them asked.

"Prison," he told him.

"Shit. We had a fucking ex-con working for us with our women there, Lenny. I can't believe you let him stay," the second one whined.

"Shut up. How was I supposed to know he was a convict?" The one called Lenny hit him hard in the stomach.

They took turns beating him. When one of them got tired, the next one took over. None of them were in that good of shape considering they should have been working a garden, but with four of them taking turns, he wasn't doing too well.

The sound of another vehicle approaching where they were located didn't seem to bother the men. They continued hitting him until a gunshot had them all scattering. A second shot sounded, and the four men scrambled for the truck, pulling out in a cloud of dust and slinging gravel as they left him there tied to the tree.

"What the hell?" A man's voice sounded fairly near, but Granger didn't have enough strength to lift his head and open his swollen eyes, if he even could, to see who was talking.

"They worked you over good, man. Let's get you cut down." The man cut through the ropes, taking most of his weight when he was finally free. "Can you walk? You're big enough. I'm not sure if I can carry you or not."

"Walk," he managed to get out.

"Sounds good to me." The stranger put his arm around Granger's waist and helped him walk toward the man's truck. "Need to get out of here before they decide to come back. Hold on while I open the door."

Granger leaned against the side of the truck while the other man cleared him a spot. Then the other man helped him up into the cab, closing the door after he was settled. Granger let his head fall back against the seat. He could feel the blood dripping from his nose, mouth, and a cut over his eye. He didn't have the strength to wipe it off.

"Here you go." A wet cloth went to the cut over his head. "Hold it while I drive. Once we get somewhere that I think we'll be safe for a little while, we'll get you cleaned up. Might need stitches to that place on your forehead."

"It'll heal," he said.

The other man grunted. "Want to tell me what that was all about?"

"Stopped them from beating some kid for stealing a rotten tomato to eat. They didn't like it."

Again, the man only grunted. Neither of them spoke again. Granger let the hum of the road noise lull him into a light sleep. It occurred to him that he didn't know the name of the man who'd rescued him. He'd ask when he woke up again.

* * * *

Destiny shivered as she curled up under the blankets she'd found in the chest in the old cabin she was staying in. Her body ached from all the bruises she'd gotten when they'd beaten her. If the stranger hadn't intervened, they'd have killed her. She was positive of that. She owed him her life, but she doubted she would ever see him again. Leaving in the middle of the night had been the safest thing to do. She couldn't leave with him and take the chance that he found out she wasn't a boy. Men couldn't be trusted when it came to women. There were so few of them left that guys went crazy when they were around them.

No, it had been for the best that she'd left when she did. It didn't matter that something about him made her want to trust him. He was strong and very masculine. Even the terrible scar across his face didn't stop her from liking the way he looked. The one thing she regretted was that she didn't know his name.

He had a magnificent body, standing at about six foot three inches. He probably weighed close to two thirty. Although she hadn't been able to tell much about his body since he wore a coat most of the times she saw him, the few times she'd noticed when he was chopping wood, she swore he had muscles on top of muscles. She had wanted to run her hands under his shirt and feel every inch of his chest and shoulders. Because of that, she'd steered well away from him whenever possible.

As she lay curled up, she imagined how he looked with his coal-black hair that had been just long enough that he was able to pull it back while he worked. The inky blackness of his eyes gave her the impression that he didn't miss anything. That was one of the reasons she felt like traveling with him would have been a mistake. He would have figured out that she wasn't a boy.

The few times she'd heard him speak, his deep rumbly voice had stirred up things deep inside of her that had no business being interested. At twenty-two, Destiny was a virgin and had no intentions of ever being otherwise. Some of the things she'd seen while she'd been traveling still made her sick at her stomach. Men were cruel and nasty when it came to wanting sex. She could do without—would do without it.

She tried adjusting how she was lying to ease the ache in her ribs, but it only seemed to stir the pain up more. She didn't think they were broken, but they sure hurt like they were. She'd been horrified to see a bruise that looked like the shoeprint of one of their boots where they'd stomped her on the chest. Destiny had been forced to remove the wrapping that kept her breasts flat due to the pain. Until she could rewrap herself, she would have to stay there. She couldn't venture out without being wrapped.

She'd been lucky to find the cabin. Not only was it in fairly good shape, but it had not been ransacked or stripped of useful items like the canned goods she'd found. She could easily hide there for a week or two to heal and rest. By her calculations, she was about fifteen or twenty miles into South Dakota. She wasn't nearly far enough away from the bastards who'd beaten her, but it was the best she could do for now.

As she lay there, she drifted in and out of a fitful sleep. She'd wanted to light a fire in the fireplace, but fear that either the chimney would catch on fire or those men would see the smoke and find her kept her from attempting it. So she huddled beneath the extra blankets on the bed and slept.

The sound of the door flying open jerked her wide awake. Destiny barely stopped a scream from escaping her mouth. The men stopped just inside the door and stared at her. She recognized one of the men as the one who'd been at the farm with her. What had happened to him? His face had been beaten black and blue. The other man she didn't recognize at all. He was helping the other one stand up by the looks of it.

She watched as they slowly eased over to the couch. The man from the farm sat down with a loud groan. The other man backed over to the door and closed it, never taking his eyes off of her.

"We aren't going to hurt you. We just needed a place to rest. We didn't realize someone was already staying here. We'll move on as soon as the storm blows over," the stranger said.

"You're the kid from the farm. Why'd you run off?" the one on the couch asked.

Destiny was too scared to say anything at first. Finally, she had to know what had happened to him. She drew in a deep breath, remembering to keep her voice pitched low at the last second.

"What happened to you?"

"Those friends of yours didn't take my stopping them from killing you very kindly," he said.

"I–I'm sorry."

He sighed and winced when he tried to rub his face. "Not your fault. They're bullies and assholes. How are you doing?"

"I'm okay. Just needed to rest for a while." She turned her attention to stranger.

He sat on the arm of the couch just watching her. His wavy brown hair didn't quite reach his shoulders and the warm chocolate of his eyes belied the expression on his sharp facial features. Right then, he wasn't happy about his situation. She couldn't help wondering who he was and why the guy from the farm was with him.

"My name's Marty. What's yours?" he asked.

"D–Dusty," she said, almost forgetting not to use her own name.

"I'm Granger," the other man said. "Where are you headed?"

"Got family somewhere in Montana. I'm hoping to find them," she said.

Destiny felt very uncomfortable sitting in the bed with the covers up around her neck. She was fully clothed underneath, but she didn't have her chest wrapped. They'd notice if she didn't stay covered.

"Guess we're all headed in the same direction, then," Marty said. "There's safety in numbers. Let's stick together for now. Since I have a truck, you'll get there faster with me. Right now, we all need some rest. Have you eaten, Dusty?"

She nodded her head, too nervous to say anything now. How was she going to keep her secret if she stayed with them? But how could she pass up the chance to ride and get to Montana much sooner with less chance of danger?

"I'll fix us something to eat, Granger. Why don't you bunk down with Dusty, and I'll take the couch. I'm a little shorter than you are, so I'll fit better." Marty picked up the pack he'd dropped by the door and rummaged through it until he had located a couple of cans and a can opener.

Destiny panicked when Granger pushed himself unsteadily to his feet and headed toward the bed. She quickly scooted to the very edge on one side, leaving the other two-thirds of the bed to him.

"Hell, I'm not going to bite you, kid." Granger dropped heavily to the bed and kicked off his boots. "You're not my type, and I'm too fucked up right now to be of any danger."

Destiny could hear the slur to his words and realized he'd had something to drink, probably to ease some of the pain. His face looked like it hurt, but then hers wasn't a lot better. She didn't say anything to that. She just turned on her side, leaving her back to him and closed her eyes, praying that sleep would soon claim her.

Chapter Four

Destiny opened her eyes the next morning feeling slightly better. She had rested well, despite the unusual circumstances. Her aches and pains were just as bad as the day before, but somehow getting more sleep had made it all easier to handle. She eased out of the bed, careful not to wake her bed partner. She needed to take care of nature's call and brush her teeth. If it was at all possible, she needed to wrap her breasts as well.

She made it outside without alerting anyone and took care of business. After brushing her teeth and rinsing with the bottled water she'd brought with her, Destiny stepped back inside the cabin and carried her pack into the bathroom. After several false starts, she finally managed to get the wrapping back around her chest. Once her eyes stopped watering, she returned to the main room to find Marty up going through his pack.

"Morning, Dusty. Have anything against making a fire?" he asked.

"Wasn't sure about the chimney. Didn't want it to catch on fire." Destiny glanced over to where Granger groaned and turned over in the bed.

"Valid point. I'll check it out. If it looks clean enough, we'll start one," he said.

She watched as he put everything back into the pack in an orderly fashion, then set it aside. He carried a lantern over to the chimney to investigate it. After a few minutes of looking around and up the flue, he grunted and headed toward the door.

"I'm going to have to climb up on the roof and make sure there's nothing blocking the top. Otherwise, it looks safe enough." He walked outside and closed the door behind him.

"Where'd Marty go?" Granger asked, sitting up with an obvious wince.

"Up on the roof to make sure the chimney's safe to start a fire in the fireplace," she said.

"Hmm," he said.

Destiny walked over to where he sat on the side of the bed. She noticed the stitches above his right eye for the first time. It bothered her that he'd been hurt because of her.

"I'm sorry they did this. You shouldn't have stopped them."

"They'd have beaten you to death, Dusty. People like that have no morals, no stop button."

"I know, but you wouldn't be hurt now if you'd just walked away." She couldn't let it go.

"Yeah, well, what's done is done. How are you feeling? You're moving awfully stiffly."

"I could say the same about you," she said with a small smile.

He stared at her for a long time. It made her nervous, so she ducked her head and studied her feet. Finally he spoke again.

"They caught up with me in a clearing about an hour away from their place. I didn't have a chance with all four of them concentrating on me. After they tied me to a tree, they took turns beating me. Marty pulled up with the intention of grabbing a quick nap and saw them. He shot over their heads a couple of times and scared them off. Then he cut me loose and half carried me to his truck. I suppose what goes around comes around. Now we just need to watch for our chance to return the favor to him." Granger's unexpected explanation of what happened to him surprised her.

Even more, his matter of fact acceptance of it made her rethink how she thought of him. He didn't say much, but he'd left her alone. And when she had been in trouble, he stepped in to help, knowing it would mean that he lost a place to crash. Instead of being bitter and angry about the beating he'd ended up getting, he shrugged it off and didn't hold it against her. More and more, Destiny was falling under his spell, and that scared her. She couldn't afford to like, much less trust, anyone, especially a man.

The sounds of stomping above them had them both looking up just as a light shower of dust and debris rained down on them.

"Fuck!" Granger brushed the stuff off his face then cursed again when he touched the swollen areas around his eyes.

"Wait. I'll get something to wipe it off." She hurried over to her bag and grabbed a clean cloth then wet it with her water bottle.

She stood between his legs without thinking about it and gently cleaned his face, making sure get the grit out from around his eyes and the cut over his eyebrow. When she finished, she realized how intimate her position was and quickly backed away. She deepened her voice as she walked over to the other side of the cabin.

"Should be fine now."

She could feel Granger's eyes on her. Her aching breasts reacted, despite being constricted beneath the binding. Her nipples down right hurt. She could feel her juices gathering and worried that they would smell her. She had to get hold of herself before she gave herself away. Staying with them wasn't going to be an option no matter how much safer she felt. Sooner or later they would figure out her secret.

"Thanks." Granger's gruff voice startled her. She just nodded and hung the cloth up to dry.

The return of Marty through the door was a welcome distraction. She listened as he filled them in on the condition of the chimney.

"It looks safe enough. I didn't find any birds' nests or anything stuck in it. The roof around it is stable enough. I think we can have a fire without needing to worry overly much." Marty started setting up the wood he'd brought in with him.

"So, Dusty. Where are you from?" Marty asked.

She realized he was talking to her and had to clear her throat to answer. "Um, Atlanta. Was living with an aunt and uncle until they died in a fire."

"Tough luck. What made you decide to head west all on your own like this?" he asked as he lit the kindling.

"Got cousins living in the Montana area. Didn't have anyone back in Atlanta. Seemed like a good idea at the time." Destiny tried to keep her answers short and to the point like men tended to do.

"Well, we're not far from there now. Another two days and we'll be crossing the border. We could probably make it in one, but I'd rather take it slow and be careful. Too much danger out here to go off halfcocked." Marty stood up as the fire caught and blazed.

Immediately the cabin began to warm. It had been so long since she'd had a fire that Destiny had to resist going up and putting her hands out to warm. It wasn't winter yet, but it would be soon. While it was still quite warm during the day, the nights got chilly. When it rained, it got chilly.

"How are you feeling this morning, Granger?" Marty asked.

"Hmm, fine. Beat to hell and back, but I'll survive. I've got some jerky in my pack if you guys want some." He nodded over to where his pack rested by the door.

Destiny felt guilty for having taken all the cans of food from the cabin earlier. She slowly walked back to her pack and pulled out a couple of cans and held them out to Marty.

"Found them here when I crashed. We can open them and share," she said.

Marty nodded and got busy preparing a meal of sorts with her cans of vegetables and Granger's jerky. They ate in silence at first. Then Marty and Granger talked about the next stage in the drive to Montana. She couldn't help but think it was odd that all three of them were heading to the same state. What were the odds of that?

"What about you, Dusty? That sound okay to you?" Granger asked.

She looked up to find both men staring at her. "S–sorry. I guess I wasn't paying attention."

Heat rose in her face. She hated that she blushed so easily. It wasn't natural for a man to do that.

"We figured we would stay here another day so you and Granger can recover some more then head out early the next morning. We'll drive 'til about three in the afternoon and stop at the first safe-looking place that we find for shelter for the night," Marty said.

"Sure. That sounds good to me." She still wasn't sure she was going to stick with them.

Evidently Granger sensed that because he stared hard at her before adding, "You're not planning to go off by yourself again, are you? It's not safe for anyone alone out there, and you're sort of small to be out on your own."

"I can take care of myself." Destiny almost forgot to keep her voice low.

"Not saying you can't, but you have to admit there's safety in numbers, son," Marty said.

She held her tongue when he grasped her shoulder in a firm grip. The heat from his hand seeped through her shirt into her skin, causing a warm rush of sensation to flow over her. What was wrong with her? Why did the touch of these two men affect her so? True, she'd never been around men other than her uncle until she'd ended up on her own, but she'd been around plenty since then. None had ever made her female parts go soft and wet like they did with these two men.

Destiny couldn't travel with them. She'd give herself away for sure. It hit her hard that she wanted them, wanted them like a woman wants a man with sex. That alone scared the crap out of her, but add to the mix that it was two men and not just one, and Destiny almost couldn't stop the shakes from taking over.

"I'm going to look around outside. I'll gather more kindling while I'm at it." She stood up too fast and winced at the pull on her ribs.

"Don't wander far. Watch for wolves," Granger said in his gruff voice.

She just nodded and grabbed her pack. A good walk would help her clear her head of all the hormones pulsing through her bloodstream. Opening the door, Destiny stepped outside and closed the door behind her. She needed to pay close attention to where she walked so she didn't get lost and let someone or something sneak up on her. She grabbed a sturdy-looking limb to use as a walking stick and stepped into the woods.

* * * *

"He's been gone a good while. I'm worried about him. He's just a kid," Granger said.

He and Marty were sitting in chairs pulled up in front of the fire. They'd been talking about their lives before that year. When Marty had told him that he'd been a cop before everything went bad, Granger felt like he needed to admit he was an ex-con. He told him the truth of what had happened, but he hadn't expected the other man to believe him. Strangely enough, Marty said he did and seemed to be serious about it.

"He'll be fine. It's only been about an hour." Marty looked over at him with a strange expression.

"What?" he asked.

"It doesn't matter to me none, but are you attracted to Dusty?" he asked.

Granger almost jumped up and hit the man for even saying that. Something stopped him though. He stopped his head in mid swing.

"Hell, I don't know. I've never liked men that way. There's something about the kid that's, I don't know, appealing. I'm not attracted to you even a little bit. Doesn't matter though, 'cause I'm not about to act on it. He's barely legal."

Marty chuckled. "There's no such thing as legal or illegal nowadays, Granger. Thanks for not being attracted me—I think."

Granger just shook his head. "It's more like I want to take care of him. Keep him safe and, I don't know. Just hold him. I'm not really getting a hard-on for him or anything. Fuck. That's screwed up all in itself."

"Don't sweat it. It makes you human and just proves to me that you're a good man, regardless of your past." Marty stood up and stretched. "I'm going to walk around. I'll see if I catch sight of the kid while I'm out."

Granger just nodded and relaxed back into the chair, letting the heat from the fire soothe his aching muscles. What he wouldn't give for an honest to goodness bath. He could easily enjoy a nice long soak in a hot tub of water. It didn't bother him one bit that it sounded more like something a woman would think about. Hell, cowboys in the eighteen hundreds looked forward to bath day just like the women did.

It pissed him off that he was questioning his manhood now. Even if he did like Dusty that way and was attracted to him and all, it didn't mean there was anything wrong with him. It was just something about Dusty that brought this out in him. That was all. With a sigh, he closed his eyes and drifted off to sleep.

The sound of the door slamming back against the wall jerked him from sleep. He stood up so fast that he was dizzy for a few seconds. The sight of Marty carrying an unconscious and bleeding Dusty into the cabin snapped him back into his head right quick though.

"What the hell happened?" he yelled as he closed the door behind them.

"Heard a gunshot and found him lying on the ground, bleeding like a stuck pig," Dusty said as he carefully laid the boy on the bed.

"Why would someone shoot him? I didn't even hear the damn gun." Granger took the boy's boots off while Marty removed his shirt.

"What the hell?"

Granger looked up to find Marty staring at Dusty's bloody chest. He saw the material wrapped around the boy's chest as well.

"He must already have an injury he's been keeping hidden. No wonder he moves funny," Granger said. "I'll put pressure on the bullet wound, and you see what else is wrong."

Granger took the discarded shirt and used it to apply pressure to the bullet wound in Dusty's shoulder. The kid didn't make a sound when he did. The boy's chest was underdeveloped for the amount of musculature of his arms. He watched as Marty slowly cut through the binding with his knife. When he cut through the last piece holding it together, both men nearly swallowed their tongues.

"Holy fuck! He's a girl," Granger said.

"Um, more like a woman, I'd say," Marty said.

"No wonder I've been so conflicted about him, um, her. He's a she." Granger couldn't stop the relief from filling him.

"Hell, that had to hurt to bind herself like that, especially with those bruises. I guess this is from the beating she took back at that farm you were working at," Marty said, pointing at the massive bruises covering her chest and abdomen.

"Fuck. Yeah. They were kicking and stomping on her. I should have gotten to her sooner." Granger still couldn't get past the fact that Dusty was a woman.

"Better take care of that bullet wound and get her covered back up before she wakes up and finds us staring at her breasts," Marty muttered as he pulled a sheet over most of her chest.

Granger continued to hold pressure to the wound while really looking at her face for the first time. How had he missed it? She was obviously very pretty, despite the whack job she'd done to her hair. She had delicate features that had helped her appear younger than she probably was. With breasts like hers, she had to be at least twenty or so, at least he hoped so. His earlier attraction to Dusty as a boy had exploded into full-out lust over her as a woman. He didn't think he could handle being this attracted to someone under eighteen or nineteen.

Marty returned with supplies, and together they worked on removing the bullet and cleaning her up. Once they had a bandage covering her shoulder, they dressed her in a new shirt and settled her in the bed.

"We don't have a clue who shot her or why. We need to get moving as soon as possible," Granger said.

"I agree, but we can't move her for at least twenty-four hours. We've got to give that wound time to start healing, or she'll keep bleeding." Marty shrugged.

"We'll need to keep watch and take turns sleeping. I've got my rifle and a box of shells, what about you?"

"I've got my Sig-Sauer and my BUG, an S&W 637 J-frame. Got plenty of ammo for now," Marty said.

"You rest first while I keep watch. If she wakes up, she knows you a little better than she knows me." Marty set up next to the window that looked out over the front.

There was a window over the sink, and another one on the opposite wall near the bed. All of them had curtains covering them. Marty would move from window to window while he had watch. Granger kept his rifle on the bed next to him just in case. As he settled down next to Dusty, or whatever her name really was, Granger prayed she wouldn't freak when she realized they knew her secret. He also prayed that whoever had shot her was long gone and wouldn't be giving them any more trouble.

Despite it still being light out, it wasn't long before he relaxed enough to fall asleep. He dreamed of Dusty and her beautiful breasts.

Chapter Five

Destiny hurt all over, but especially her left shoulder. It felt as if someone had stuck a hot poker to it and twisted it round and round. She fought to open her eyes to figure out what was wrong, but they refused to open right away. She searched her memory of why she felt like this, and it all came rushing back. She gasped, and her eyes flew open.

Immediately she knew something else was wrong as well. She could breathe easily for a change. That meant her binding had been removed. And that meant they knew she wasn't a boy. Fear poured over her like wet paint, sticky and thick. She started to sit up so she could run, but a hand gently pressed her abdomen back onto the bed.

"Easy, honey. You're safe. Just relax so you don't hurt yourself." She stared up into Marty's warm eyes. "No one is going to hurt you."

"What happened?" she asked, looking from him over to the window where Granger stood with a rifle in his arms.

"Someone shot you. Do you remember seeing anyone?" Granger asked.

"No. The last thing I remember is picking up kindling to bring back." She reached up to touch her shoulder, but Marty stopped her.

"You'll hurt yourself," he said.

"Did you get the bullet out?" she asked.

"Yeah. You're going to be sore as hell for a while, though." Marty sat up on the edge of the bed.

"Y–you know about me, don't you?" she finally said.

Both men looked at her with solemn faces and nodded.

"It doesn't matter, Dusty. We aren't going to hurt you. You're safe with us," Marty told her.

"Destiny," she said. "My name is Destiny."

"That's a pretty name." Granger's deep voice and the way he spoke were like a calming balm to her splintered nerves.

"Why would someone just shoot me for no reason?" Destiny felt a small measure of relief not to have to pretend around them anymore.

"Don't know. We're going to need to leave as soon as we can move you. It's obviously not safe here." Granger looked out the window again.

"Let's go now." She started to get out of bed, but Marty stopped her.

"You don't need to move around for the next few hours. Need to give the wound time to start the healing process, or you'll just start bleeding again."

"I'm just going to make you two sitting ducks if we don't leave now." Destiny hated being a burden to anyone, especially to these two men who'd been kind to her.

"We're safe enough for now. You lie back down and rest," Marty said with a frown.

"He scowls better than you do," she said before she realized what she was going to say.

Granger chuckled from across the room. "She's right. Your best mean look so far is just a stern-looking frown. Bet you had a hard time staring down bad guys as a cop."

"Fuck you." Then, as if realized they had a woman present, his face grew red. "Sorry."

She frowned up at him. She didn't like that now that they knew she was a woman and not a teenage boy they would treat her differently. Instead of saying something about it, Destiny closed her eyes and tried to rest. Unfortunately, now that she was awake and knew that she'd been shot, her shoulder hurt more than the beating had.

After thirty minutes of trying to find a comfortable position between her aching ribs and her shoulder, Destiny gave up. Before either man could stop her, she sat up with her back against the headboard.

"Why didn't you let one of us help you? You're going to reopen the wound and make it start bleeding again," Granger fussed. He stuffed a pillow behind her back then drew the covers up.

"I can't be still. The damn thing hurts worse than that beating did." She knew she was whining, but she couldn't help it.

"I'm sorry there isn't anything to give you for the pain," Marty said.

"Wait. I've got some whisky. That'll dull the pain some." Granger rummaged through his pack and came up with a metal flask.

When he opened it and tried to hold it to her mouth, Destiny growled and grabbed it from him.

"I'm not an invalid. I can manage to drink by myself." She turned it up and took a large sip.

When it started down her throat, she thought it would burn a hole all the way to her bones. It took a second before she could even manage to gasp for breath.

"It's stout stuff. You need to go easy on it," Granger said with a smile.

"No kidding," she managed to gasp out after a few seconds of sputtering.

"Just take a small sip every few minutes, and it will start to dull the pain. Don't drink too much, or you'll just make yourself sick and end up screwing up your shoulder when you throw up tomorrow," Marty added.

Destiny had no intentions of getting drunk and suffering a hangover. She'd observed the men do that in some of the towns she'd been in when looking for supplies. She wanted no part of getting sick enough to throw up her toenails.

An hour later, Granger re-capped the bottle and put it away. The pain in her shoulder had died down to a dull throb when she moved it. Her bruises didn't even exist any longer as far as pain went. The pleasant floaty feeling carried her into the night when Granger stretched out next to her on top of the covers.

"Aren't you cold?" she asked with a slight slur.

"I'm fine. Go to sleep, Destiny. Marty said you should be up to moving tomorrow. You need to get some rest."

"But it's cold in here. Get under the covers so you'll be warm."

"That's not a good idea. Go to sleep."

Destiny pouted. She wanted him under the covers so she could scoot closer to him. She could feel the heat from his body and thought it would be so much nicer to be able to snuggle closer. With an exaggerated sigh, she closed her eyes and tried to settle down to sleep. After what only felt like a few minutes, Granger whispered in her ear to wake up but not to make a sound.

"What is it?" she whispered back.

"Someone's outside moving around. We might have to make a run for it. I want you awake and ready," he said.

Marty eased away from the window and crouched next to the bed. "There's two of them. Take a look through the window, Granger, and see if you recognize them."

Granger eased off the bed and silently walked over to peek through the window. After a few seconds, he pulled back and nodded in their direction. Once he had returned within whispering distance, he confirmed that they were the guys from the farm they'd left.

"There can't be more than three of them. I can't imagine they would leave the two women without someone to defend them," Granger told them.

"If we stay here, we're sitting ducks. We need to get to the truck and haul ass," Marty said.

"I agree, but how are we going to manage that without them picking us off? I only saw two of them, but that doesn't mean there isn't another one sitting out there in a tree or something waiting for us to show ourselves." Granger stared from her to Marty.

"Our best bet is to sneak out as soon as night comes. We can go out the window over there since it's opposite from where we've seen the men. Waiting until night will give us an advantage. Unless they have night vision goggles, they won't be able to see us well enough to shoot accurately." Marty waited to see what they were going to say.

Destiny wanted to tell him it was too dangerous, but she knew that sticking around where they were was just as bad. They couldn't stay there forever, and what would happen if they decided to burn them out? No, leaving was their best option. She'd just have to suck it up so she wouldn't slow them down. Now that they knew she was a woman, they'd make allowances for her. She didn't want that. It would put them all in danger.

"I think you're right. We need to move as soon as we can," Granger said.

"Destiny? Think you can make it to the truck? We're going to need our hands free in case we need to use our guns," Marty said.

"I'll be fine. Just tell me when to run." She would make it if it killed her.

"That's the spirit." Marty turned and nodded to Granger. "More than likely they plan to wait until they think we're asleep to attack. We need to catch them off guard and run as soon as it's full dark."

Destiny cringed at the thought of one of them getting hurt because she was too slow and they slowed down to keep her safe. She liked both of them too much for that to happen. The fact that she cared for Granger had begun to sink in, but realizing that she'd already started to have similar feelings for Marty scared her. It wasn't normal to feel this way about two different men.

She tried to blank everything out of her head so she could be ready when Marty said it was time to go. There would be plenty of time to worry about feelings and how right or wrong they were once they were safely on the road again. It looked like she was going to be traveling with them for a while now anyway. It would give her time to heal so that when she went her own way, she would be able to take care of herself once again.

* * * *

Marty stared out the slit in the curtains, making sure nothing was moving. He wasn't sure this was a good idea, but it was the best one he could come up with. Truth be known, he didn't expect them to make it to the truck. It wasn't that he was afraid of dying, but it pissed him off that he had let a bunch of assholes like those guys get the drop on him. He should have been expecting them to try something. If they'd driven farther away, they wouldn't have bothered to follow them, but since he'd stopped so soon to give Granger some time to recuperate, it had been too good of an opportunity for them to pass up.

To make it worse, they had a woman to protect now. It didn't matter that they hadn't known earlier that she wasn't actually a teenage boy. The fact remained that she was supposed to be protected, and he'd screwed up.

"Anything moving out there?" Granger asked in a low voice from his position across the room.

"Don't see anything. Should be able to head out in another twenty minutes." Marty pulled on his backpack.

"Just say the word. I'll have Destiny up and ready when you do."

Marty nodded without saying anything as he continued to focus all of his attention on the area out front that he could see. It was as if the sun sank in slow inches instead of seconds as time was usually measured in. When he could no longer make out the outline of the porch railing, he eased away from the window and stood up. Turning, he nodded at Granger.

The other man already had his backpack on and quickly helped Destiny out of the bed. When she started to slip on her own backpack, Granger stopped her.

"You can't wear it, or you'll irritate that wound and start it to bleeding again," he said in a soft whisper.

"I'll wear it over one shoulder. You've got to have your hands free in case you need to use your rifle," she reminded him.

"Don't put it on your injured shoulder, Destiny. If you open that wound back up, you'll end up with an infection. You're lucky as hell you haven't so far, anyway." Granger helped her settle the pack on her right shoulder.

"I'm ready," she said.

Marty watched her, worried that she wasn't doing nearly as well as she appeared to be. She was a strong woman. He couldn't help but admire her. Very few women he'd known in his life would have had the guts, much less the ability, to fool people into thinking she was a young teenage boy and work their way across the states with the world all fucked up like she had. No, she was a woman to be treasured and taken care of.

He carefully opened the window, making sure once more that nothing seemed to be moving, before slipping out to stand guard while Granger helped Destiny climb through. He kept his body between her and the surrounding woods while Granger climbed out next. Together, the three of them made their way deeper into the trees. He saw one of the men who'd been watching the cabin up in a tree not far from them. The idiot lit a hand rolled cigarette, announcing his location like a lighthouse strobe light. He made sure to check the trees after that, winding them around behind the idiot smoking.

They kept low and used any bush they could locate as cover. He was thankful that Destiny knew how to be careful walking to keep the noise down. Marty took them in a zigzag pattern to make it more difficult to follow them if they had somehow picked up a tail. He didn't think they had, but he wasn't leaving anything to chance.

Finally, they reached the spot he planned to leave them to go grab the truck. It amazed him that they'd managed to get away without a fight. Stealing the truck out from under them was going to be tough.

"Okay, you two stay here. Right through there is the road. I'm going to get the truck and bring it back here. As soon as you see me stop there, get in fast."

"Marty, it's too dangerous. Leave the truck. We'll make it fine on foot until we find another one," Destiny said.

"Darling, you're not going to be able to keep up with that bullet wound in your shoulder. Besides, we need the ammunition and supplies in my truck." Marty looked over her head at Granger. "Keep her quiet until I get back. If you hear anything, or if I don't show up in twenty minutes, run and don't look back."

"Watch your ass, man. We'll be here waiting on you," Granger said.

"Marty…" Destiny started to speak again.

"Shh, or you're going to give away where you are. I'll be back." Marty slipped back into the darkness.

He took a much more direct approach back to grab the truck than he had getting them to a safe hiding place. As soon as he was within sight of the vehicle, Marty made a circle to try and locate where everyone was located. He made out one more man hiding on the opposite side of the cabin as the one in the tree. Neither one of them would be able to see him climb into the truck. The third man worried him. He had no idea where he was. That meant he had one chance to grab the truck and haul ass.

He had long ago removed the light in the cab of the truck that came on when the door was opened. He could open the door without making a sound, but if he closed it, the noise would give him away. No closing the door until he was on his way out. The next thing that might lead to his getting himself shot was if they'd thought to disable the truck. That would make him a sitting duck.

He checked his watch. Eight minutes down. He had to hurry. Sweat dribbled down his back. More of it traced a path down the side of his face.

A brief flash of the moon light off something shiny caught his attention, and he realized where the third man was hiding. In the damn truck bed.

Fuck! What am I going to do now?

Chapter Six

Time seemed to drag as they waited for Marty to make it back
with the truck. Each second pounded away inside of her, taunting her
that they were in this mess because of her. If she hadn't eaten that
damn rotten tomato, none of this would have happened in the first
place.

"Easy, woman. I can hear you worrying from here. He'll be fine."
Granger's low voice barely registered in her ear.

"I'm sorry, Granger."

"For what?"

"For getting you and Marty in this mess. If it wasn't for me…"

"Stop that right now," Granger bit out. "None of this is your fault.
They were using us to keep from having to do their own damn work
and not feeding us enough to keep a dog alive. More than likely they
have bodies buried out there somewhere from the people they've had
working for them over the years that finally starved to death."

She shivered at the thought of that. She wouldn't put it past them,
either. Though she'd never met the two women living inside the
house, she wondered if they were there by choice or if they'd been
captured and were being held against their will. It was that very fate
she'd been running from.

The sounds of gunshots echoed through the woods, making her
jump. Terror that something had happened to Marty tightened her
throat until she felt as if she were choking. Only Granger's large hand
on her uninjured shoulder stopped her from jumping up and running.

"Hold on. Marty will be here," he whispered.

One minute, then two, ticked by before the sound of a vehicle gunning the engine reached their ears. Again, Granger's hand kept her in place. When the truck pulled up exactly where Marty had said he would, Granger let her stand up but kept her behind him as they slipped through the bushes.

Marty threw open the passenger side door. "Hurry up. We've got to get out of here before the other two follow us."

"What about the third man?" Granger asked as he jumped in after her and slammed the door.

"Don't look in the back. We'll have to dump the body after we've lost them," Marty said, a grim expression on his face.

Destiny realized that he'd had to kill one of the men to get the truck to them. She could tell it hadn't been something that he'd been comfortable doing, despite the fact that they had tried to kill her and would have killed them given half a chance. It made her admire him even more that he didn't take any life lightly.

"Where are we going now?" she finally asked.

"Soon as I'm sure they've given up on chasing us, we'll look at the maps and decide our next step," Marty said.

"Do you think they'll give up after one of them got killed?" Destiny was afraid they'd chase them down until they caught them.

"Yeah, they'll give up soon. They have two women back at their farm, from what you've told me. They aren't going to want to leave them with only one man to watch them. Besides, winter will be coming soon, and they still have a lot of work ahead of them to get ready for it." Marty flashed a tight smile at her before returning his concentration to the road.

"Destiny, lean back and relax. We've got a long night ahead of us." Granger settled their packs in the floorboard.

"We need to look for a larger truck when we stop as well," Marty said.

"Yeah, don't think you were expecting two passengers when you started out." Granger chuckled.

"There's safety in numbers, man. Safety in numbers." Marty kept glancing in his rearview mirror as if he expected someone to pop up in the back of the truck.

Destiny sighed and tried to relax, but her shoulder ached something fierce. Knowing there was a dead man in the bed of the truck didn't help either. When Granger attempted to stretch out some, he laid his arm along the back of the seat so that his arm brushed the back of her head. Even that small amount of contact had her blood heating. She clamped down on the desire that began to rise, reminding herself that she looked like a survivor from a refugee camp. He wouldn't be the least bit interested in someone like her.

Though that thought helped dampen the effects of having both men so near to her, it did little to make her feel better. She had no experience with boys, let alone men. All of her knowledge of the opposite sex and about sex in general came from the many books she'd read over the years. She'd been lucky in that her aunt and uncle hadn't been super conservative. They'd supplied her with romance books that got progressively more explicit as she grew older.

She could remember her aunt saying, "Dessie, baby. One day we'll find a good man for you, and you're going to want to know what to expect and how to please him as well as take your pleasure from him."

She had known how wonderful they'd been to her, but she hadn't known how hard it had been for them to provide for her without anyone knowing about her. She had great clothes, the books, and plenty to eat. How they had managed to do all of that without getting caught, she didn't know. She missed them so much.

At some point she must have fallen asleep, because the next thing she knew, the sun was coming up and they were pulling in to a parking lot somewhere. She blinked, trying to clear the sleep from her eyes.

"Where are we?"

"We just crossed into South Dakota. We've been driving parallel to Montana for a few miles," Granger said.

"Why are we stopping here?" she asked, yawning.

"Time to switch trucks," Marty explained. "You and I are staying here while Granger finds us another set of wheels."

She watched as Granger got out of the truck, carrying only his rifle. She wanted to tell him to be careful, but she wasn't sure if that would jinx him or not. Right then, they needed every bit of luck they could get. When she turned to ask Marty how far they were from the Montana border, the way the rising sun hit his face made her stoop and swallow. He was a beautiful man, all hard planes and angles. Right then, there were dark circles under his eyes, a testament to how little sleep he'd had in the last twenty-four hours.

"As soon as he gets back with a truck, you need to let him drive, and you need to rest. You're exhausted," she told him.

"I'm fine. Once we're on the road again, I'll rest." Marty kept looking around, one hand on his weapon, and the other on the steering wheel.

"Where are we going after this?" she asked. Now he had her looking around as well.

"I'm not sure, yet. I want to find a safe place to spend the night tonight so we can all rest. We'll look over the maps then and decide together." He looked down at her and smiled a smile that looked so tired to her. "Don't worry, Destiny. We'll keep you safe."

She smiled back at him with more confidence than she felt. "I know you will."

Less than five minutes later, the sound of an engine drawing closer had Marty pushing her down in the seat.

"Don't move until I tell you it's safe. We don't know if there's anyone else around here or not."

Destiny tried to remain still, but her shoulder ached from crouching down in the seat. With their packs in the floorboard, there wasn't room to get down there. She waited as the motor drew nearer.

She saw the second that Marty knew it was Granger by the way his shoulders relaxed.

"Okay, you can sit up now." He opened his door and climbed down. "Scoot over to this side to get out, Destiny."

She scooted over, letting him help her down from the truck. Granger was stepping out of a fairly new-looking brown Jeep Patriot four-by-four with a smile.

"Couldn't have picked a better one than this. It has almost a full tank of gas, heated seats, and will probably take us just about anywhere we need to go. Plus, it has covered storage, which we might need." He hurried around the other truck and grabbed their packs.

"Climb in, Destiny. We need to make a few more stops before we get back on the road," Marty told her.

She climbed into the backseat and buckled up with some help from Marty. Her left arm wasn't much use for anything other than making her shoulder hurt. She watched him grab things from behind the seat of the old truck, handing them to Granger, who put them in the back of the Jeep. He climbed up into the back of the truck, but she couldn't tell what he was doing. She could barely make out his expression, but it was enough to know he wasn't comfortable being back there with a dead body. Destiny had almost forgotten that there was a dead man riding around with them in the back.

After handing several things to Granger, Marty jumped down from the truck and climbed in the front passenger seat of the Jeep. Granger settled their packs on the back seat next to her. Then he got in behind the wheel and closed the door. Seconds later, they were driving away from the old truck. She wasn't sure how she felt about leaving the body there instead of burying it. Despite the fact that the men had been trying to kill them and that one had actually shot her, it seemed wrong to just leave him there.

"If it had been safe to do it, Destiny, we would have buried him. It just isn't safe," Granger said. How he'd known what she was thinking, Destiny didn't know.

They rode through the small town without seeing anyone in the area. Where she'd come from in Atlanta, there were always people milling about during the daytime. She'd watched them with a pair of binoculars, wanting to see what others looked like besides her aunt and uncle. The farther west she'd traveled, the fewer people she saw. Right after everything had gone crazy, everyone left had flocked to the cities where they thought they would be safer and have better access to food and water. Instead, it had led to disease, and a second outbreak of different plagues swept through those areas with the greatest concentration of people.

Now, those who were smart and able to make the journey were returning to the west, away from all of the crime and disease that still festered there. Her aunt and uncle had wanted to do that, but neither of them thought they would be able to work a garden and handle the primitive living conditions at their age. It was what she knew they would have wanted her to do if something had happened to them.

Granger pulled up in front of a general store of some kind, jumping the curb and stopping just shy of the already wide open doors.

"Don't know if there will be anything left we can use, but right now, we need a lot of things," he said as he climbed out.

Marty opened the door for her to get out. In the end, he'd had to help her down. Her shoulder hurt enough that she was slightly nauseous, but she wasn't going to say anything.

"Stay close to one of us, darling," Marty said.

She followed close behind as both men entered with their guns pointed forward. Sunlight barely reached into the front part of the store, but Granger had brought a lantern with them. He led the way as they ventured deeper into the silent building. The shadows thrown around from the lantern swinging in Granger's hand creeped her out.

"If you see any clothes you need for cold weather, grab them," Marty told her.

She kept between the two men, afraid to leave their sides. She caught sight of some coats thrown over a rack that looked her size. She tugged on Granger's shirt and pointed toward them.

"Yep, they look like they might fit you. Try them on until you find one that will work." He held the lantern up for her.

She drew in a deep breath and grabbed the first one that she could reach. It was obviously too small. She tossed it back on the rack and grabbed another one, nearly screaming when a second one dropped on her at the same time.

I'm losing it. I've got to calm down. They aren't going to let anything happen to me.

The second coat fit snuggly, but the one that had dropped on her was perfect. She kept it on and followed Granger as he and Marty picked through things, finding them jeans, long-sleeved flannel shirts, and even thermal underwear. Marty made two trips back to the truck with their findings before Granger called an end to their hunt.

"We need to find a pawn shop or something that hasn't been emptied to get more ammunition," he said.

They drove around several blocks before he located one set back off the street that looked like it hadn't been touched. He had her stay in the truck while he and Marty made sure it wasn't occupied and broken into. Then they let her follow them inside.

It was a wonderland of survivalist gear, including guns and ammunition. Knowing how important all of this stuff was, she didn't even make fun of them when they acted like kids in a candy store. Even she was smiling when they finished loading the Jeep with everything from MREs to matches. After they had stuffed everything they could in the jeep, the two men closed up the building so that it looked as if no one had been inside. Going so far as to remove the pawn shop sign as well.

"Why did you do that?" she asked when they climbed back in the vehicle.

"It will keep people from just trashing the place, since it looks like no one's been there, and it will keep things safe for others who really need it. Plus, if we end up back this way again, maybe it will still be there for us if we need supplies again," Granger explained.

They made one more stop at a grocery store where they were still able to find a few cases of canned goods in the storage area in back that hadn't been taken. She also found some first aid supplies in the employee area. Marty found a sling to keep her arm stationary, so she'd quit jostling her shoulder trying to use it out of habit.

"I think we've done all the damage we can here," Marty said. "Time to move on and find a spot to sleep and plan."

Thirty minutes later, Marty slept in the front seat, a soft snore drifting back to her every once in a while. He had to be totally exhausted. She was worn out, and she had slept much more than they had. She caught Granger watching her in the rearview mirror.

"What?" she asked, keeping her voice soft.

"How are you doing? Is your shoulder hurting?"

"It's sore, but I'm fine."

He frowned. "Don't lie to me, Destiny. We can't afford to."

"It hurts, Granger, but I can handle it." She wanted to cry now. Somehow acknowledging that it hurt made the pain worse, made the entire situation worse.

He nodded and didn't say anything for a long time. She watched out the window as they drove through dense woods, then open fields that had grown wild. Some of the road was obscured by the overgrown vegetation beginning to brown. She couldn't believe how wild it seemed out there. As a child, she'd always heard how there were no more wild places in the US anymore. Man had taken over every useable inch, leading to the extinction of many animals from the destruction of their natural habitats. Even the once protected national parks had lost valuable lands and funds toward the end.

During all the reading she'd done over the years, and with all the time she had to do nothing but think while she educated herself,

Destiny had wondered if the disasters had all been nature's way of fighting back and taking back her land, returning it to the way it had been before man had devastated it. Looking around her now, she could very well believe it.

Nearly two hours had passed when Granger spoke up, startling her from her thoughts. She jerked, jarring her shoulder in the process.

"What are you thinking about so hard back there?" he asked.

"I don't know. Just wondering if everything that's happened was nature's way of cleaning house. I mean, when an animal population gets too large for an area, disease thins them out or a bad winter will kill off the weak. How is that any different than what happened seven and eight years ago?" she asked, watching his eyes in the mirror.

He met her gaze for a few seconds, then returned it to the road. "I don't know. Maybe you're right."

"Man had overpopulated most of the nation. We lived on top of each other in the big cities, dug up whole forests to build more houses or grow more food. Maybe all of the destruction finally hit a nerve in the Earth's center that caused everything to go haywire at once."

"Either that, or God got tired of man and his arrogance and decided to stop holding back the disasters that everyone kept predicting were going to tear the world apart." Granger's eyes seemed thoughtful.

"Maybe so. All I know is that someone got pretty pissed off and took it out on us. I hope they're happy with everything now and will leave us alone."

Chapter Seven

"Marty, wake up." Granger shook the other man's shoulder.

"What's wrong?" He straightened up, instantly palming his weapon as he did.

"Nothing. I think I found a safe place to hole up for a day or two."

Marty blinked and looked over in the backseat. "She been asleep long?" he asked.

"No, about an hour is all. I'm going to go in and check it out. I didn't want to leave with you asleep." Granger climbed out of the Jeep, the lantern in one hand and the rifle in the other.

The place in front of him was a small house that looked to have been owned by an older couple. Though there wasn't a car or truck in the drive, he wasn't taking chances that someone was inside and would take a shot at him. He knocked on the door, using the old fashioned knocker someone had hung. When there wasn't any sign of someone moving around inside, he tried the door knob.

Locked.

With a sigh, he tried looking in the mailbox without any luck. He searched under the welcome mat, but there wasn't a key there either. He was just about to break the window by the door when he spotted the flower pot with a very dead plant of some type in it. He picked the pot up and sure enough, there lay the key.

He unlocked the door and carefully walked inside. The smell of a house closed up for a long time nearly choked him. It didn't smell like old death, as if there were bodies somewhere that had decomposed in the house, just dusty, old house smell. They could open the windows for a few hours and air it out enough to be able to stand it.

As he made his way from the entrance hall to what must have been the living room, he noticed that it looked as if pictures had been removed from the walls. There were outlines here and there punctuated with nails. Whoever had lived there had packed up and left. He felt better about searching the house knowing that. He didn't think he would stumble on a skeleton anywhere now, especially with there being an absence of the smell of decomposing flesh.

The kitchen looked pretty much untouched. He wasn't about to open the fridge, though. Few people in a hurry would have taken the time to clean out their perishables. He turned down another short hall and found two bedrooms. The first one looked like a guest room that, other than dust, didn't appear to have been used much. The next room was the master, and here the evidence of flight could be seen. Drawers were left pulled out, most empty, but some still held the remnants of someone's life.

The closet was wide open, with empty hangers lying on the floor amid a pile of discarded clothes and forgotten shoes. He held the lantern higher to make sure there wasn't anything in the room that could be dangerous, then he checked the bathroom in the hall. The house was empty. It would do for a short stay to regroup and make plans.

When he emerged from the house, he could see that Destiny had woken up. She was talking with Marty. He blew out the lantern and opened the Jeep's door.

"Looks like it will be fine. I'm going to put the Jeep under the carport. There are plenty of canned goods for a few days, so all we need out of here are our packs and weapons, I think." He climbed inside and started the engine again.

Once all three of them were inside, he felt better. Granger didn't like being separated for any length of time now. It struck him as funny that only a few days ago, he'd scoffed at the idea of having to deal with anyone else, preferring his own company as much as possible. Here he was now, worried about leaving two near strangers alone for all of fifteen minutes.

"I think we all need to stay together in the master," Marty said, echoing his own thoughts.

"Why? Aren't we safe here? I mean, there are good locks on the doors," Destiny said, looking very nervous at the prospect of sleeping in the same room with them.

"Sweetheart, anyone can break a window and come in. The locks on the doors wouldn't have kept us out," Marty pointed out.

Granger watched her shiver. Her reluctant nod reminded him that she was the one in the most vulnerable position. They needed to sit down and have a very serious talk as soon as they had everything set up.

"Marty, I'll grab the food and some things to eat with. You and Destiny set up the bedroom for safety. Take the lantern with you." He held it out to Destiny.

When she took it, their fingers touched, and a spark danced across their skin. He heard her gasp, and he managed to keep the torch from dropping when she snatched her hand back. Marty took it from him with a frown.

"Are you okay, Destiny? Did you hurt your shoulder?" he asked.

"No, just shocked myself. I'm fine." She kept her eyes down, not meeting Granger's, as she turned to follow the other man down the hall.

Granger wasn't sure what that had been, but it hadn't been static electricity. There was no reason for a buildup that would have resulted in a discharge between them. The only explication he could come up with had to do with attraction, and that sure seemed a little far-fetched to him. If he didn't know better, he'd have wondered if he'd read too many romance novels while he'd been in prison. He grunted and walked into the kitchen to grab what they would need for a meal.

Ten minutes later, he eased down the hall toward the light flickering in the back bedroom, carrying a tray he'd found with three plates, three sets of utensils, a can opener, various cans of vegetables, and three bottles of water. He'd found an entire case in the bottom of the pantry. They'd be sure and carry that with them when they left.

"There you are. We were beginning to wonder if you'd decided to eat by yourself." Marty's voice held a thin line of strain in it.

Granger set the tray on the dresser and looked from Destiny to Marty, trying to figure out what was going on. Nothing on their faces gave him any clues as to what might have been the cause of the tension in the air.

"Let's eat, and then we need to talk," he said.

"What about?" Destiny's quick response said she already had a good idea and didn't want to have that conversation.

"Food first. Conversation second," he repeated.

Once they'd finished the meal of green beans, baby whole potatoes, and sliced peaches, Marty loaded everything back on the tray and took it back to the kitchen. Granger watched as Destiny fidgeted where she sat on the foot of the bed. He didn't say anything, waiting for Marty to return. This conversation needed to happen with everyone in the room at the same time.

He looked around and noticed that they'd moved the chest of drawers over in front of the window to help block it in case someone tried to get in. They could shove the dresser in front of the bedroom door when they got ready to sleep. He figured it was a pretty good plan, and he prayed that it really wasn't necessary.

"I wiped off the plates, so we can use them tomorrow." Marty walked back into the room.

"Let's sit on the bed where it's comfortable and talk." Granger kicked off his boots and climbed onto the king-size bed and leaned back against the headboard.

Marty followed suit, taking the other side of the bed. Destiny merely turned around, scooting a little closer to them. Even in the dim light of the lantern, Granger could see how nervous she was by the way her eyes darted around, and she kept her right hand buried in her lap so they wouldn't notice how much she was shaking. He hurt for her. She had to be scared to death as a woman alone in a man's world now. She was trapped with two men she barely knew who could hurt her at any time. They needed to be careful around her. If she spooked and ran, she would end up in a much worse situation. He wasn't going to let that happen.

"W–what did you want to talk about?" she asked.

"We need to talk about you, Destiny," he said. He hoped that by making it about her and giving her choices, she would be more willing to accept them as her protectors.

"Me? What about me?" She stiffened, her chin going up.

"You've done an amazing job of making it as far as you have all alone, honey, but it's not safe for you alone out here. You can trust us to keep you safe, but that has to be your decision. We can't keep you safe if you don't trust us and let us do it," he said.

Marty nodded. "We'd never do anything to hurt you. But if you don't do what we say, when we say to do it, it will put your life and ours in danger. We have to trust you as much as you have to trust us."

"Why would you help me? What do you want from me?" she asked, the knowledge in her eyes of what she was worth to them.

"Because you're a woman alone and in danger. We don't want anything to happen to you," Marty said.

"Because I think we could be a family, given time to get to know each other. Because a woman isn't safe with just one man anymore. Out here, most families are made up of two or more men to each woman. Marty and I want to take care of you together." Granger glanced over at the other man, hoping he would go along with what he was saying.

They hadn't really talked about it in so many words, but they'd skirted around the subject enough while she'd been sleeping that he felt fairly sure the other man was on board with the idea. At least he hoped he was. Granger was attracted to Destiny, and he had been even when he'd thought she'd been a boy. Now that he knew she was a young woman, the attraction had developed into a raging wildfire.

"I promise you that we will do everything we can to make you happy, Destiny. You don't have to jump to a decision right now. We're going to be traveling another few days looking for a community that we feel comfortable in," Marty assured her.

"What we do need now, though, is your willingness to trust us with your safety. We need to know that you'll do what we say without argument. We wouldn't tell you to do something without a very serious reason. Can you do that?" Granger asked, his fingers crossed in his head.

She didn't say anything right away, and he could see that her eyes were almost glazed over in shock. He hadn't anticipated that she'd be affected like this. He'd actually thought she would get angry and accuse them of just wanting to get her into bed with them, but this hadn't been his intention.

"Destiny, honey? Look at me. Nothing is going to happen. We aren't going to force you into anything." He looked over at Marty for help.

Marty looked just as confused as he felt. He scooted down the bed toward her. She jerked back so fast that she fell off the bed backward.

"Fuck! Her shoulder," Marty shouted as both of them jumped down and hurried to the foot of the bed.

Destiny held her arm and used her feet to scoot away from them. Even in the dim light, he could see tears streaming down her cheeks. They'd scared her and caused her to reinjure her shoulder at the same time. What a fucking mess.

"Easy, honey. We aren't going to hurt you. Let Marty check on your shoulder, baby." Granger stayed back while the other man eased closer to her.

"We're not going to hurt you, darling. I promise, we'd never hurt you," he said again.

She stared from one man to the other as she started shaking all over. Hell, she was going into shock. She'd been through too much already, and he'd just delivered the straw that broke the donkey's back suggesting she embrace them in a ménage relationship.

"Marty, she's crashing, man."

"I've got her," the other man said as he reached her as she passed out. "Hell, her shoulder's bleeding."

Granger stood up and swept the sheets to the foot of the bed so Marty could lay her on the bed.

"Grab the first aid kit, Granger." Marty quickly removed the sling.

When Granger returned with the first aid kit and some towels, Marty had removed her shirt and was dabbing at her shoulder with it. Granger moved the lantern closer so he could see better.

"Is it okay?" he asked.

"She opened it back up some, but not too bad. It's not infected so far. I'm going to clean it up again while she's out. It will probably wake her up because it's going to hurt like crap. Get ready to hold her down if she comes up swinging." Marty took some gauze and poured alcohol over it. Then he laid it over the wound.

Sure enough, she came up swinging, trying to dislodge Marty then Granger. She screamed loud enough to wake the dead. Granger covered her mouth with one hand and tried to calm her down at the same time.

"Easy, Destiny. Marty's trying to stop the bleeding again. You reopened your wound. Settle down, woman." His voice got gruff with emotion. He hated seeing her this way.

Her eyes seemed focused now, though wide with fear. He slowly released his hold on her mouth and then her other shoulder. Her chest rose and fell at a rapid rate as she fought to catch her breath. When she looked down to see what Marty was doing, she evidently realized she was exposed from the waist up and threw her good arm over her breasts.

"Here, honey. Let's cover you up now." Granger eased a towel over her breasts, leaving her left shoulder uncovered. "Is that better?"

She nodded but didn't say anything. He could see that she was still unsure as to whether she should trust them or not. He didn't want to give her any reason to decide she couldn't. Granger backed away while Marty finished dressing her shoulder. As soon as he had, he, too, moved back from her.

"I'm going to get something for you to wear to sleep in, Destiny. I'll be right back," Marty told her before he left the room.

She continued to stare at him with suspicious, wide eyes while they waited on Marty to return. When he walked back in the room carrying an overly large T-shirt, she visibly relaxed. Some of the tension between his eyes loosened enough that he thought he could breathe again.

"Okay, I'm going to thread your arm through the armhole first. Then you can put your other arm in, and we'll pull it down over your head. Try to keep your left shoulder still if you can," Marty told her. "Granger, help me here."

Granger moved in slow motion to the bed, afraid he'd startle her again. This time she didn't move, but she did watch his every move as he helped the other man dress her in the giant shirt. After they had pulled it down her body, Marty pulled the towel out from under the shirt.

"There, now. I bet you feel better, don't you?" he asked.

She nodded her head, her eyes drooping with fatigue. He and Marty covered her up, and they walked over to the bedroom door. At Marty's nod, they stepped outside into the hall to talk.

"What the fuck? You scared her to death, man." Marty's voice was tight with anger.

"I know. I guess I thought that since she was handling everything so well that she would be okay with talking straight about everything. I mean, she's been taking care of herself, has taken a beating, and got shot. I didn't expect this to be too much for her." Granger felt like a heel.

"Apparently it was. I don't think she's all that worldly, Granger. I mean she's, what? Twenty-three or so?"

"Yeah. I was just trying to be honest and up front with her." He was the older man, and he had totally screwed this up.

"You didn't even talk about this with me. Why did you think you could just speak for both of us, anyway?" Marty asked.

"We'd sort of discussed it. I thought you were okay with it. I'm sorry, man. I really thought talking about it with her was the right thing to do."

He couldn't see the other man's expression in the darkness of the hall. Without the lantern, he couldn't see his hand in front of his face. Somehow it seemed dirty and sinister to be discussing sharing her in the dark like this. They couldn't leave her alone unprotected, so this was the best they could do.

"Look. I'm all over protecting her. Hell, I'd love to be her man, but I'm not so sure about the sharing part. I mean, that's an awful lot to ask of a woman who's been through what she's been through. Hell, any woman."

"Marty, that's the way things are out here. The dangers are real that someone will try to take her. It takes more than one man to keep a woman safe. I'm not being kinky about this or anything. It's just the way things are now." Granger realized that the other man thought he was just looking for a threesome.

"You're saying there really are other families out here living like that?" Marty's voice sounded doubtful.

"Yeah. Pretty much every one I came across when I was moving around was set up that way. Some were made up of three or four men and one woman. It was all consensual, too. Not like that farm where Destiny and I were working." Granger waited as Marty seemed to digest what he'd told him.

"What sort of dangers are we talking about out here? I was thinking that if I moved out here, the only things I had to worry about were wild animals and nature."

"Besides the wolves, bears, and such, there are black market agents looking to steal women to sell on the black market and to Barter Town. Women are treated like slaves there, chained up and sold to the highest bidder, or turned into brothel whores. It's safer than back in the cities, but it's still not safe." Granger wanted to return to the bedroom to watch over Destiny. He didn't like there being a door between them with so much danger out there.

"How is this supposed to work? Do we take turns or something? That just seems weird." Marty still didn't sound totally convinced.

"I guess it depends on how we want it to work. Actually, it all comes down to what Destiny wants. Keeping her happy and safe is the most important thing. Without her on board, it's a moot point anyway." Granger sighed. "Look. Let's just agree that we both want to keep her safe and go from there until she's had time to think everything through."

"I agree. Until she's okay with it, we're just beating ourselves over the thinking about it. We need to get some rest." Marty opened the door to the bedroom and slipped inside.

Granger drew in a deep breath to calm down the inner turmoil coiling inside of him. He wanted Destiny safe, and he wanted to see her happy. It confused him that he cared so much about her after so little time. It had to be that the intense situation they had found themselves in was the cause of it. Stress did strange things to people. Right now, they were all safe. That was what was important. Marty was right. They needed to rest while they could. Then they needed to decide on a direction and a course of action.

He couldn't help but wonder how Destiny would act in the morning. Her perception of everything would set the tone for the rest of their trip.

Chapter Eight

Destiny came awake with a start. Not only did her shoulder hurt, but her head ached as if she'd hit it at some point. She didn't remember bumping it on anything. Light sifted in around the chest of drawers sitting in front of the window, dust motes dancing in the beams. As she watched them, she became aware of the fact that she wasn't alone in the bed. When she turned her head slightly, she could see the outline of one of the men lying on his side, his back facing her. She could tell by the length and darker color of his hair that it was Granger. When she turned her head to the other side, it was to stare into the warm brown eyes of Marty.

"Morning. How are you feeling?" he asked quietly.

"Um, okay, I guess." She wasn't sure what to say next. Thankfully, Marty took pity on her and spoke again.

"What about your shoulder? Is it hurting much?"

"Not too bad. It's going to hurt some until it's fully healed. The sling helps." She broke eye contact and looked around the room.

"It's early yet, Destiny. Try and sleep a little longer," he said.

She closed her eyes, but sleep was far away now. Instead, she started talking, her eyes still closed.

"Was Granger serious last night? Do you two really want to s– share me?" she asked.

He sighed. "Destiny. We can talk about this later. We don't have to do anything about it at all. We both just want to make sure you're safe. Let it go for now."

She knew she should, but something inside of her was too curious now. She needed to know.

"But do you want to share me, Marty?"

"I don't know, Destiny. I like you. A lot, but sharing someone seems so wrong. I mean, I wasn't raised that way. I'm not sure how I would handle seeing another man touching what I considered to be mine. Does that make sense?"he asked.

"Yeah. I don't get it either. How can a relationship work with two possessive men and one woman? I can't even imagine there being more than two. It has to be really hard to negotiate something like that and everyone be happy with it." Destiny opened her eyes and realized that Granger was awake. He'd turned over at some point, and she hadn't even felt the bed shift.

"Hey," was all he said, but she could see the guilty expression marring his face.

"Morning," she replied.

"How did you sleep? Did your shoulder bother you any?" he asked.

"Not enough to wake me up. I slept all night, I guess." She gave a small smile, then turned her head to look above her at the ceiling. "Where do we go from here?"

"We get up and eat something. Then we plan out which direction we head. That's it, Destiny. Nothing else."

"Are you hungry?" Marty asked her.

She started to shake her head no, but her tummy growled and everyone laughed, breaking the tension that had built until she hadn't been able to take a deep breath.

"Stay in bed until we get something ready. I don't want you moving that shoulder around for now," Marty said as he got up.

She quickly averted her eyes when she realized he wasn't wearing anything but a T-shirt and boxers. She didn't look in Granger's direction at all when she felt that side of the bed move as he got up as well. Some things she was better off not seeing right now. Her head was in too much turmoil to add thoughts of them wearing next to nothing to the mix.

While they dressed and moved the dresser away from the door, Destiny contemplated what Granger had said the night before. At the time, she'd been so keyed up from the last few days that she hadn't been able to deal with it. Now, after a good night's rest, she realized that she needed to give it serious thought. Since she'd never really had a normal relationship with a man before, she had nothing to compare what he'd been suggesting to. Outside of her aunt and uncle, she only had memories of her life before the disasters to fall back on.

She wasn't going to deny that she was attracted to both men. Even though she knew that normal was only one man and one woman, that had been before and this was now. Life was different now. There were very few women, and there were men out there who thought nothing of taking her for their own reasons without thought to what she wanted. Despite the fact that she'd only known them for a short time, Destiny knew in her gut that she could trust them. She accepted that they wanted to keep her safe.

So where did that leave her with Granger's proposition? She sighed, still confused.

"Here you go, darling. Breakfast in bed." Marty grinned, setting a tray on the bedside table.

"Let me help you sit up, little one. I don't want you to hurt your shoulder." Granger knelt on the edge of the bed and gently pulled her up while Marty arranged two pillows behind her back.

"How's that?" Marty asked.

"Good, thanks." She watched as he arranged the tray on her lap and opened a bottle of water for her.

"Don't expect this type of service all the time, young lady," he said with mock severity.

She pouted, playing along with the light teasing. "But I'm worth it."

Granger and Marty exchanged glances, and Granger smiled, a warm seductive heaviness to his eyelids. "That you are, little one. That you are."

Destiny shivered and turned her attention to the food in front of her. It wasn't fancy, but there was plenty of it. She glanced over to be sure the men were eating as much as they'd given her. Satisfied that they weren't skimping to be sure she had enough, she quickly devoured the meal. Last night had been her first full meal in a long time. This one she enjoyed with just as much enthusiasm. Going without had taught her a valuable lesson. Eat when you can, because you never knew where or when your next meal might come.

"That was good. Thanks, guys." She wiped her mouth with the cloth they'd given her.

"You're welcome, ladybug," Marty said with a smile.

"Sit tight while we clean up, then we'll spread out the map and start making plans." Granger grabbed the tray and eased off the bed.

Ten minutes later, they sat around the little kitchen table with the map spread out between them. Marty had pulled back all the curtains, so they had plenty of sunlight to see by. Granger had produced a pen and circled their present location to the best of their knowledge.

"This is two twelve. It will take us all the way into Montana," he said. "This is where I met the first lot of settlers that I worked for. They were nice enough but very nervous of strangers. Besides, I really think we're better off going a little deeper into the state."

"I agree," Marty said. "When I talked to people on the road, they all said the farther west you went, the safer you were."

"Let's steer clear of the main interstates as much as we can. Too great a chance that we'll run into trouble on one of them. I think we should keep to these county roads until we reach Broadus, where we can pick up two twelve." Granger traced his finger along a line that connected with the road he wanted to get on.

Destiny looked over the map and the route he planned to take. It looked like it had been well planned out in advance.

"I think we can find a place to rest at Broadus, then move on toward the Cheyenne Indian Reservation. There were some families living there as well. Most were Native Americans, and they were prepared for anything. Many of them still believed that the government was going to try and kick them off their land again and had made sure they had plenty of supplies." Granger leaned back in his chair.

"So we stop in Broadus next. Why don't we head farther north?" Marty asked.

"Couple of reasons. One is that we want to stay away from the larger cities where the most dangers are, like Miles City. Billings is out of the question. I think we'll be okay in the little towns. The other reason is the farther north we go, the harder the living conditions. They get snow year-round farther north. It would be harder to grow a garden and keep food on the table."

"So where exactly do you see us ending up?" Marty asked.

Destiny was wondering the same thing. The more Granger talked about the dangers, the less certain she became that she'd made the right decision.

Granger pointed at a spot on the map over half way across the bottom of Montana. It looked like it was right above Yellowstone to her. Why would he want to take them into an area that was rife with wildlife?

"This is where I think we have the best chance. There aren't nearly as many people in this area, but it has enough of a summer season we should be able to have a decent vegetable garden," he said.

"That's near Yellowstone," she pointed out.

"Some of the best deer and elk hunting around will be there. We'll need the meat and skins in the winter. I'm not sure how many communities are set up in that direction, but I know there are some on the way. If we feel comfortable around any of them and they'll accept us, we can always settle down there." Granger looked from her to Marty. "Do we have a plan?"

"It sounds good to me," Marty told him. "What do you think, Destiny?"

"I–I guess. Yellowstone scares me. You know that with it being a national park that there are a lot more wild animals there than anywhere else in Montana."

"We still have a ways to go before we reach there. Let's take it one step at a time." Granger gently touched a finger to her chin.

"Okay. So what's next? Do we pack up and go?" she asked.

"Not today. We'll head out early in the morning. Today we rest," Granger told her.

"You're only waiting because of me. I'm fine. I can travel." It irked her that ever since they'd found out she was female, they had been treating her differently.

"It's as much for us as it is for you, ladybug," Marty told her. "We've been going nonstop for a long time. We need some rest so we'll be at our best to deal with anything that comes up on the road."

"If you say so," she muttered as she stood up and headed back to the bedroom.

"Hey, where are you off to?" Granger asked.

She stopped and looked over at him. "I was going back to the bedroom. I thought you wanted me to *rest*."

He chuckled. "Don't get sassy with me, little girl. We're going outside to get some fresh air and explore a little bit to see if there's anything else here we might be able to use."

"Keep close to us and do what we say without arguing, Destiny, okay?" Marty said.

She was so happy to be doing something other than sitting in the bed, she nodded immediately. Both men laughed at her instant agreement. It wasn't like she was agreeing to obey their every command or anything. She shivered, and her nipples hardened beneath her shirt. Why did that make her hot? It was ridiculous what seemed to turn her on.

"Okay, let's go." Granger had his rifle and had emptied his pack, as had Marty.

"Do I need to get my pack?" she asked.

"No. We're just carrying these in case we come up with something we want to bring back. Besides, your shoulder is still healing." Marty dropped a quick kiss to her forehead before turning her to face the door where Granger stood waiting on her.

The two men kept her between them everywhere they went. She wasn't allowed to go off even two steps away from them. It was kind of cute at first, but it didn't take long before she was aggravated. What could happen to her five steps away?

They located another house some thirty minutes later. Granger stomped up on the porch and knocked on the door to make sure there wasn't anyone inside.

"Hello? Anyone here?"

No one called out, and they didn't hear any movement inside. Granger shoved open the door and eased inside. She and Marty waited outside while he made sure it was safe. Several seconds later he stuck his head out the door.

"Come on in. Looks like someone was stocking up, but no one's been here for a long time. There are spider webs everywhere. Be careful where you walk. There's been squirrels or raccoons living in here at some point. Stuff's all over the place." Granger disappeared back inside the house.

Marty helped her up the steps so she didn't lose her balance with her arm in a sling. When she walked into the dimly lit room, she started coughing at the dust in the air. Granger had stirred it all up just walking through the mess on the floor. Newspapers and stuffing from pillows had been shredded and piled up in different places. No doubt they were old nests for something. She didn't want to look in them to find out in case there was anything still lurking.

"What a mess," Marty muttered under his breath.

"Yeah. Don't fall over something." Granger had cleared off the table and set his pack on it. "Let's load up what we can and then come back for the rest."

Since she wasn't carrying anything and couldn't reach a lot of the cans, Destiny wandered around the little house while they gathered what they wanted to take back. They were going to pile the rest on the table to make it easier to pack up on the next trip.

There was only one bedroom and one bath across from the living area. The bedroom held nothing but men's clothing. Judging by the size, he'd been on the small side. When she found a picture in a drawer of an older man and probably his wife, she figured the house had belonged to him. He looked about the right size to wear the clothes. She couldn't tell that anything had been taken. There were no empty hangers or spots in the drawers like he'd packed up and left. The bathroom appeared untouched as well, with an old fashioned shaving brush and mug along with a razor sitting on the counter.

She searched beneath the counter and came up with a very nice first aid kit. She carried it back into the kitchen. The men were stacking the last of the provisions on the table.

"What did you find?" Marty asked.

"First aid kit. Looks like an old man lived here alone. There weren't any women's clothes, so he must have been a widower. A picture showed a man and woman in their sixties," she said.

"Guess he took off when things got bad out there." Marty said.

"I don't think so. He didn't pack any clothes or toiletries if he did. Nothing's missing," she explained.

"That's weird. Makes you wonder if something happened to him while he was out somewhere," Granger said. "Let's go. I want to have time to make a trip back to get the rest of this stuff."

They left the cabin with Granger closing the door behind them. The trip back to their house was uneventful and much faster. Granger had her resting while they unloaded their packs, then after a quick meal of beans and water, they hiked back to the house to finish appropriating the supplies they'd found.

"Don't wander off, Destiny," Marty said when she told them she was going to sit on the front porch.

The dust inside was killing her allergies and making her eyes itch. She brushed off the chair, and after making sure it would hold her weight, Destiny sat down and looked around at the overgrown yard around the house. The gravel drive was almost obscured with weeds. She listened absently to the guys' low murmurs as they worked. Something glittered in the grass just off the side of the porch. She got up and walked over to see if she could tell what it was, but she didn't see it from there.

Destiny walked back over to the chair, and sure enough, sunlight bounced off of it from that angle. She kept her eyes where she'd seen the sparkle and stepped off the porch to see what it was. When she got to that spot, she bent down and picked up a metal box of some type. Most of it was still shiny. It was only about three or four inches square but rattled when she shook it.

"What did you find?" Marty asked, stepping out of the house onto the porch.

"I don't know. It's a box of some kind. I wonder why it isn't covered in rust. Look, most of it's still shiny." She held the box up.

"Bet a raccoon tried to carry it off and dropped it. I'm pretty sure I read somewhere that they like shiny things," Granger said as he closed the door to the house behind him.

"Well, I'm keeping it. I want to see what's inside once we get back to the house." She started to walk toward the front of the house where the porch steps were and heard a low growling noise.

"What was that?" Marty hissed out.

"Don't move, Destiny." Granger's voice held enough worry in it that she froze on the spot.

Chapter Nine

Again the animal growled, only louder this time. Destiny realized it was coming from under the porch. Sweat broke out over her body at the continued growl and chuffing noises coming from less than three feet away.

"What the fuck is that?" Marty asked.

"I don't know. It sounds like a cross between a bear and a wolf. There isn't enough room under the porch for a bear. I'm not sure about a small wolf though." Granger eased a few steps closer to Marty. "Destiny, honey. Don't move. Don't give it any reason to come out."

"I'm not moving," she whispered.

Destiny wasn't sure how she was even breathing right then. Raw fear had her frozen to the spot. If they decided she needed to run, she wasn't sure she would be able to make her legs move.

"I'm going to walk over there, Destiny. Just stay calm and be ready to move if I tell you to, honey," Granger said.

"Wait." Marty stopped him. "How good are you with that rifle? I mean, are you a really good shot with it or not?"

"I'm good." He looked at Marty for a brief second then nodded. "You're right. I need to be ready to shoot if it attacks."

Marty nodded and stepped off the porch. When the animal didn't make another sound, Granger stepped off right behind him. They both walked slowly around the front of the porch toward Destiny. Granger walked in a wider circle than the other man. When Marty was about five feet from her, the growling started again, so he stopped.

"How are you doing, ladybug?" he asked.

"Okay." It came out in a whisper as if she couldn't get enough air inside her lungs to speak louder.

"Granger?" Marty said the man's name, but nothing more.

"I'm in position. Just don't either of you move toward the porch. Destiny. Take one slow step toward Marty."

"I–I don't think I can move."

"Sure you can, honey. Just look at me. Look right at me." Marty held out a hand toward her.

Destiny tried to move but couldn't make her muscles unfreeze. They felt as if they were glued solid so that she couldn't bend at all. The animal was silent right now, and that was a good thing as far as she was concerned. If she moved, he'd start growling again. No, she didn't want to move.

"Move, Destiny!" Granger bit out in a deep growl.

She began to pant as she slowly forced her leg to relax enough she could bend her knee and move a step closer to Marty. She was in the middle of taking another step when the growls became more ferocious sounding.

"Stop!" Marty yelled.

"It's going to bite me, isn't it?" Destiny cried out as she tried to stop the shaking from taking over.

"Shh, honey. Calm down. Just take a deep breath and blow it out. We're going to get you out of this. Listen to us and do exactly as we tell you to. It will be fine." Granger's voice no longer sounded uncertain or worried. She leaned on that strength and slowly stopped shaking.

"Good girl. Now slowly take one step closer to Marty. Only one, Destiny," Granger said.

She slowly moved one foot closer to Marty and stopped like Granger had said. No sounds emerged from beneath the porch. Maybe it had moved farther under the house, or maybe it was even escaping on the other side.

"Okay, take another step toward Marty. Only one, Destiny."

She closed her eyes and settled her nerves before taking one more step away from the porch. Again, all was quiet. She was tempted to go ahead and run to Marty, but Granger had said to only take one step. She was going to follow his directions. He'd promised to take care of her.

"Good girl. You're doing a great job, Destiny. Now take another step toward Marty for me, baby." Granger's voice held a soothing tone that kept her nerves quieted when all she wanted to do was run screaming into the woods.

"Okay. Now one more step, and he'll have you, Destiny. One slow step."

She stared into Marty's eyes, willing her foot to move. She took one last step, and Marty pulled her into his arms and turned all at the same time. She heard the enraged growl behind them as Marty sprinted toward the woods, giving Granger a clear shot. They were depending on him to stop whatever it was from getting to them.

The crack of the rifle firing jarred her hard enough she nearly fell from Marty's grasp. His hands bit into her skin in an attempt to hold on to her. Another shot, and the world around them was silent. Marty continued to run until Granger's yell to come back stopped him.

"Are you okay, ladybug?" he asked.

She buried her head in his neck trying hard not to cry in relief. She knew she was hurting her shoulder, but she couldn't let go of him for anything right then.

"Destiny? Honey. Talk to me." Marty's voice took on a worried note.

"I'm okay. What was that?" she asked in a shaky voice.

"I don't fucking believe it!" Granger's voice carried to them from a good fifty yards away.

Marty started walking back toward the other man. Destiny wiggled in his arms, trying to get him to let her down.

"Stop moving around before I drop you, ladybug."

"Put me down. I need to walk. My shoulder hurts."

It was all she needed to say. He immediately let her down easy and tried to look at her shoulder.

"Stop. It's fine. It just hurt like that." She wrapped an arm around his waist and urged him closer to where Granger was crouched next to what looked like a small bear or beaver.

"What is that?" she asked, keeping Marty between her and the carcass.

"I think it's a fucking wolverine," Granger said, a note of awe in his voice.

"I thought that was a TV show." She frowned at the mostly brown and black fur covering the animal.

"Look at these." Granger held up the animal's overly large foot to where five claws stood out stark against the black fur.

"Look at his teeth." Granger carefully held the animal's head up so that they could see the dagger like teeth.

"I didn't know wolverines were this far south. I thought they were mostly in Canada," Marty said.

"They have a small showing down here in the north part the US, especially in the Yellowstone area. I guess with everything like it is, they've expanded their areas now. They used to be nearly extinct at one time." Granger dropped the body back to the ground. "That thing was fucking fast. I was worried I wouldn't hit it."

"I'm sure glad you did." Destiny shivered looking at the thing. As much as she hated that Granger had to kill it, she was much happier with it dead and them unharmed.

Granger suddenly pulled her into his arms and hugged her close. He was careful of her shoulder, but he didn't let her go right away. She felt him bury his face against her neck in her hair.

"I was scared to death that thing was going to get you before I could kill it. You sure you're okay, darling?" he asked, his voice muffled by her hair.

"Yes. I'm okay. Thank you both." She looked over at Marty, who had a strange expression on his face.

Granger pulled back. "Let's get back to the house. It'll be dark in another couple of hours."

"Come on, Destiny. I want to change that bandage and be sure your shoulder is okay. It's never going to heal at this rate," Marty teased, the strange look from seconds earlier gone now.

"You two are going to think I'm a trouble magnet as much of it as I seem to bring down on you," she said only half joking.

"Nonsense. None of this has been your fault. Now keep up, ladybug, or I'm going to carry you." Marty popped her lightly on her ass.

Destiny looked over her shoulder and glared at him even as she rubbed her butt. It hadn't really hurt, but he didn't have to know that.

* * * *

Marty followed close behind Destiny, afraid for her to get too far ahead of him even if Granger was right in front of her. She hadn't been more than four feet from the porch and them when danger had nearly taken her from them. Sheesh, he hadn't realized what it would mean to be responsible for someone out here. He'd essentially been responsible for thousands of people at one time when he'd been active on the force. This was far more difficult than he'd have thought.

Then the sight of her in Granger's arms earlier had him questioning himself as well. It had felt right to see the other man holding her and taking comfort from her. Where was his sense of outrage and anger that someone he cared about as much as he'd come to care for Destiny was being held and caressed by another man? It didn't make sense.

When they made it back to the house, he ushered Destiny into the bedroom.

"Granger, why don't you load everything into the Jeep except what we need for tonight and in the morning? I'm going to redress her wound, and she needs to rest for a while before we eat." Marty started unbuttoning Destiny's shirt.

"Hey! Wait. I can do that. Turn your back," she demanded.

Granger grinned an amused smile at him and left them to start loading everything up. Marty sighed and turned his back.

"You know I've already seen you without your top, ladybug. Isn't this a little silly?" he asked.

"Don't remind me."

He could hear her moving around behind him. Then she sighed and told him he could turn around. She lay on the bed with the covers pulled up under her arms so that everything but a small expanse of cleavage was completely covered. He couldn't help but smile to see that she'd folded her jeans and shirt on the night stand. That meant all she had on beneath the covers was her panties. His cock got the picture right away.

Trying not to groan out load, Marty swallowed and carried the first aid kit to the bed and sat next to her.

"Let's get this bandage off and see how it looks. Have you felt like you've been running any fever or anything?" he asked as he gently loosened the tape holding the gauze in place.

"I don't think so. Other than aching most of the time or hurting if I jar it, I don't think anything's changed."

When he had the old bandage off, he noticed that there was some slight drainage he didn't like the color of. They didn't have access to any antibiotics. Only a few people in the larger cities could get those now. There was only one drug manufacturer still working at the moment. They'd have to make do and pray it didn't develop into a full-blown infection.

"What's wrong? You're frowning," she said with a worried expression.

"Nothing. There's a little drainage, but I think it's fine. I'm going to clean it again just to be safe. Think you can stand it, or do I need to wait on Granger to help you be still?" he asked.

"I can take it. Let's get it over with." She smiled up at him, but he could see dread edging around her mouth.

"I'll be as quick as I can. Hold on."

He watched as she grabbed the sheets in her hand and turned her face away so she didn't have to see what he was doing. Marty hated doing anything that hurt her, even if it was for her own good in the long run.

He poured alcohol onto a fresh piece of gauze then held it to the wound, gritting his teeth at the soft whimpers she was making. He had no doubt there would be tears in her eyes by now. He hated this. When he wiped at the raw wound, she squirmed, but she held her shoulder still.

"Almost done, honey. Hold on just a few more seconds."

Once more he saturated a new piece of gauze and repeated the procedure. Tears welled up in his own eyes as he dabbed at the wound then patted it dry and applied a new dressing. Once he'd finished taping it down, Marty gathered the dirty supplies and bagged them up to be buried outside. Then he kicked off his boots and lay down next to her, pulling her gently into his arms.

"I'm sorry, Destiny. I'd rather cut off my own arm than hurt you," he whispered in her ear.

She sniffed. "I know. It had to be done. I'm okay, Marty."

He held her close for a little longer until he felt her drift off into sleep. As he listened to her soft breathing, watching the rise and fall of her chest, he realized that he'd misjudged how he felt about her. He was pretty damn sure he was in love with her. How had it happened so quickly? And what did that mean in the whole scheme of things? Granger was as much a part of her as he was. He had no idea if the other man loved her or not, or if she loved either one of them, but like it or not, there were three of them.

His mind ticked around to how he'd felt back at the other house when Granger had held Destiny as if he'd nearly lost his best friend. Why had he been okay with that at the time? Was it just because of the situation? Or did he really think that the three of them could make something work between them? He should be furious about Granger holding her. He considered her to be his woman, but something inside of him acknowledged that she was Granger's, too. What in the hell was he going to do?

Assured that Destiny was fast asleep, Marty eased off the bed and carried the first aid kit along with the bag of soiled supplies to the kitchen. There he found Granger staring out the window over the sink.

"How is she doing?" the other man asked without turning around.

"Okay, I think. She had a little drainage I'm not happy about, but I cleaned it out again and rebandaged her."

"That had to have hurt."

"Yeah. I was as quick as I could be. She's asleep now," Marty added.

"Good." Granger turned around. "We need to talk, about us and where we see this going. I won't have Destiny hurt because we can't get our shit together."

Chapter Ten

"You're right. We need to talk." Marty's face showed nothing of what he was thinking in that moment.

Granger nodded and turned a chair around and straddled it. He watched Marty sit down across from him and hoped they could work things out without Destiny getting in the middle of it. He and Marty had to agree to work things out between them so she didn't feel pulled. It was the only way this kind of relationship would work.

"Look. I know this isn't something you're used to. Neither am I, but I've seen it work, and it's the only thing that will work in this fucked up world we're in now." Granger waited for the other man to say something.

Marty looked down at where his hands rested loosely clasped on the table. After nearly thirty seconds, he finally spoke.

"I'm not sure what to think, Granger. I'm pretty sure I'm in love with her. Don't know when it happened, but there it is. In my head, the idea of you touching her makes me see red, but today, when you hugged her back at the house, it didn't upset me like that. I was so relieved that you'd been there to kill that thing that it didn't dawn on me at first that you were touching someone I loved. Then worry and fear set in, and I started doubting myself." Marty looked up.

Granger could see the conflict eating away inside of the other man. He didn't know what to do or say to help him deal with it. It was something he had to come to terms with all by himself.

"She's so damn brave and smart, Granger. We both know she spent the last six years or so locked inside her aunt and uncle's home to keep her safe. She only knows what she's read. For all we know, she's still a virgin. How can we expect her to accept both of us as her, I don't know, boyfriends—men?"

"I'm not worried about that part right now, Marty. Like you said, she's a smart woman. She'll figure that out herself. What I *am* worried about is how we're going to act around her. If we show even the least bit of jealousy or act uncomfortable with the situation, she's going to doubt herself and what we're doing." Granger made sure Marty could see the seriousness in his eyes. They had to be one hundred percent together on this.

"I think you realized today that keeping her safe is going to take more than one man. Not only do we have to provide for her, but we have to watch out for wild animals and anyone who might try and steal her from us."

"And you're okay with this? You don't mind sharing her with me? Knowing I'm going to hold her and touch her?" Marty asked with a bitter smile on his face.

Granger drew in a deep breath and let it out slowly. "Yeah. I'm not saying it doesn't upset me deep inside, but I know it's the right thing to do for her. She's all that matters, Marty. Not our feelings, and not our pride."

Marty rubbed a hand over his face and looked out the window behind Granger. It was obvious how hard he was having to fight to deal with sharing her.

"I never thought I'd be end up being part of a family after I got out of prison, Marty. I didn't trust anyone. Still don't for the most part, but meeting her changed something inside of me. At first, after we figured out she was a woman, I planned to just leave her with you. I knew you'd do the right thing by her, and I didn't think I wanted any part of a family. I just planned to find a place close to some other people and settle down. Trade with them and live out my life on my own, just the way I wanted it." He ran his hands through his hair.

"Until I met her. Now I can't stand the idea that she might get hurt because there's only one of you to take care of her. At first, I told myself you'd figure it out and find someone to help you keep her safe, and that just about tore me up inside. No one besides me is good enough to help you keep her safe. That's when I knew I loved her. I don't know if it's the sort of love that people talk about, but it's something inside of me that doesn't want to see her hurt or unhappy. I want to watch her smile and hear her laugh."

Marty started laughing softly. Granger growled at him. What in the hell was the man laughing about? He'd just bared his soul to the guy, and he was laughing like a lunatic.

"What?" he snapped.

"I've never heard you talk so much before. To top it off, you're telling me that you love the woman I love and that you plan to share her with me. What part of this *isn't* funny to you, Granger?"

The man was certifiable. Maybe he wasn't the best choice for her after all. He started to get up, but Marty's next words stopped him.

"I'm scared that we aren't enough to keep her safe, but I don't think I could stand anyone but you to touch her."

"There won't be anyone but us, Marty. We'll keep her safe. That's why I think finding another family or a small community will work. We can all work together to feed our families and watch out for each other." Granger could see resolve in Marty's eyes now.

"It's not going to be easy, man," he said.

"I know, but we can make it work. We love her together, and we give each other alone time with her. There's no keeping score. There will be times she needs you more than she needs me, and then there will be times it's me she needs," Granger explained.

Marty just nodded and leaned back in the chair. "So what do we do now? Talk to her about it and assure her that we both only want what is best for her?"

"No. It was stupid of me to bring it up like some kind of business arrangement. She's a woman, and women are emotional. She needs sweet words and gentle touches. We seduce her together," Granger said.

"She's still not healed enough for much. We'll have to be careful," Marty warned.

"Always. We start off just getting her used to our touch. I suspect you're right and our girl is still a virgin, or close to it. She needs to feel comfortable with us first. Take every opportunity you can to hold her and kiss her. I'll do the same thing."

"I agree. It will be easier to keep her safe once she's used to being around us as well." Marty smiled, looking relaxed for the first time since they'd returned from the other house.

"So we're agreed? We share her and help each other keep her safe and happy?" Granger asked. He held out his hand.

Marty took it and smiled as they shook on it. Granger stood up, eager to curl up next to their woman now that things were essentially settled between them.

"Let's go cuddle up with her," Granger said.

Marty grinned. "She's not wearing anything except a pair of panties under the covers."

That was all it took. Granger stripped as he hurried down the hall.

* * * *

Destiny woke in stages. She'd been having a really good dream where Granger and Marty were both hugging and kissing her. She still felt warm all over from the way her body had responded to their dual touches. She was sure her pussy was drenched with juices. The thought of one of them noticing her aroused state both terrified her and excited her all at the same time.

She opened her eyes with a smile then promptly closed them again in shock. She slowly took inventory of each part of her body to determine where it was and what it was lying on. A mental picture confirmed what her eyes had been telling her.

Dear Lord, I'm wrapped around Marty like a freaking octopus, and Granger is wrapped around me the same way!

She opened her eyes, and sure enough, her head was nestled beneath Marty's chin, snug against his chest. Her left arm was draped across his waist so that her injured shoulder was cradled on his abdomen. And was that his leg between hers? She moaned before she could stop herself.

Granger shifted behind her. One of his arms was wrapped around her waist, and his head burrowed beneath her hair up to her neck. She could feel his warm breath caress her skin each time he exhaled. And there was no mistaking the rather large cock pressed hard against the cleft of her ass.

Nothing in all of the books she'd read could have prepared her for the way she felt right then. Words couldn't describe how her belly fluttered and her blood raced. Sandwiched between the two men felt like the most perfect place in the world that she could be. It defied all logic, but it felt right. She wanted them both and wasn't second guessing anything. The only stalling point in her path was how they would react. Well, that and the fact that she was a virgin and knew nothing of how to handle one man, let alone two.

She sighed. What made her think that two gorgeous hunks like them would even want her in the first place? She'd been nothing but trouble for them since they'd met her. No, she might as well enjoy these brief glimpses of heaven while she could. Once they found a suitable settlement, they'd drop her off with them and keep going.

"Mmm, you smell delicious, darling," Granger muttered against her neck. "Good enough to eat."

She felt her blood heat up once again, no doubt leaving her cheeks pink in the process. Did he know she was wet? Could he actually smell her?

"I agree. I vote we take turns eating her for breakfast," Marty's husky voice startled her.

"You're awake?" she gasped out.

"Awake and very hungry," Marty said with a chuckle. "Granger, move, man. You're heavy as lead."

The other man laughed and rolled off of her. She immediately missed the weight of him at her back. Before she could say anything, Marty had rolled her over, and she realized that they were all nude beneath the covers. That was why she'd been so toasty warm. It had been the body heat of skin against skin. She shivered with awareness as both men leaned over her with obvious bad intentions all over their faces.

"What?" she started to ask.

"Relax, ladybug. Just lie there, and let us make you feel good," Marty said with a devilish smile.

She tried to draw in a deep breath, but it was as if she couldn't get her lungs to expand. Calloused hands smoothed over her breasts, caressing them gently. She'd never been touched there by a man's hands before. The sensations of their fingers rubbing over her smooth flesh had her heart racing. When they pulled at her nipples, she couldn't help but grab their wrists.

"Did we hurt you?" Granger asked, concern written all over his beautifully scared face.

"Nooo. So good," she crooned, squeezing her eyes shut against the pleasure.

"Look at us, honey. Watch how touching you makes us feel," Granger said.

Destiny opened her eyes to see their desire etched into the lines around their eyes and at their mouths. Watching her watch them, they both slowly dipped their heads and closed their mouths over a nipple. Warm, wet heat enveloped the tight peaks as they swirled their tongues around and sucked on them.

"Oh, God!" She was going to explode.

They continued to touch and mound her breasts with their hands as they drew on her nipples as if they couldn't get enough of her. She couldn't tear her eyes away from the erotic sight of two heads bent over her breasts. Her body felt as if it was burning from the inside out.

She expected to see smoke rising from her as they tightened places inside of her she'd never thought about before.

She lifted her hands and dug her fingers into their hair, massaging their scalps like a needy kitten. Never had anything felt so good. Books didn't even come close to describing the zings of pleasure that shot from her breasts to her pussy. This was so much more than anything she ever imagined in her daydreams.

They slowly pulled away from her nipples, letting the tortured nubs pop from their mouths. Destiny whimpered at the loss.

Marty chuckled. "Easy, ladybug. We'll take care of you. Just relax."

"Feel," Granger added with a sinful smile.

They licked beneath her breasts then slowly made their way down her abdomen, nipping lightly with their teeth, then caressing the spot with their tongues. It felt so good and so bad all at the same time. Two men. Touching her. It was amazing.

The lower they went, the more of her covers they pulled away until finally, Granger tossed them all the way off the foot of the bed, baring her entire body to their eyes. Heat raced across her skin, turning it pink under their stares.

"You are beautiful, Destiny. So fucking pretty." Granger leaned over and licked her at the juncture of her thigh and pelvis.

She couldn't help but giggle and draw up her leg. He growled against her skin and held her flat as he kissed and licked all along her lower abdomen. Marty returned to her breasts, sucking on one while he pinched the nipple of the other one between his thumb and forefinger. Having them split their attentions across her body was unsettling. She couldn't seem to concentrate on any one spot. It was overwhelming until Granger changed positions and spread her legs with his body.

"G–Granger?"

"Shhh, darling. I'm going to kiss this pretty pussy and make it feel good. That's all. Relax." Granger blew warm air across her wet lips, sending shivers all over her body.

Marty pulled her attention back to him when he gently bit her nipple, pulling it tight as he teased the tip with his tongue. The pleasure-pain of it had her ears ringing.

Destiny jumped when Granger spread her thighs even wider and ran his tongue up her slit, right over the top of her clit.

Oh, God, that felt so good.

Marty moved higher and stared into her eyes, his chocolate-brown orbs commanding her to look at him as he slowly brushed her lips with his. Again, he lowered his mouth to hers and slowly moved his lips over hers in what she realized was her first kiss. She didn't count the smack to her forehead from earlier. This was a real kiss where his lips touched hers, and it felt good, magical even.

"So sweet, Destiny. Your lips are like the sweetest candy. Open for me." Marty licked across the seam of her lips.

She opened for him and gasped when he entered her mouth with his tongue, sweeping inside to explore there like he'd explored her breast earlier. He caressed each surface as he rubbed his tongue over hers over and over. When he sucked on hers, drawing it into his mouth, she thought she would pass out with pleasure. Her moan seemed to drive him crazy as he deepened the kiss to the point she wasn't sure she'd ever draw a full breath again.

Granger spread her pussy lips wide and buried his tongue deep inside her cunt, snapping her head back from Marty's kiss in a startled gasp.

Chapter Eleven

Something inside of her began to grow as Granger pumped his tongue in and out of her pussy, circling her clit at the end of each stroke. The burn of his fingers holding her spread wide so that he could bury his face in her juices as he thrust his tongue inside her had her squirming beneath him. This was more than she could have ever imagined.

While Marty played with her breasts, stimulating her with his gentle bites and little pinches, Granger drove her toward a burning explosion she knew she wasn't prepared for. She knew what to expect between a man and a woman from reading, but this was so much more than what she'd dreamed. This was pleasure that threatened to destroy her.

Each rasp of his tongue near her clit tightened her cunt until she thought she'd die from the anticipation of what was to come. His tongue licked and teased her pussy. He sucked on her nether lips, then backed away and blew his hot breath over the wet folds.

"Please, Granger. I need," she whispered.

"I know, sweetness. God, you taste like spicy honey. I can't wait to taste you when you come for me." Granger renewed his attack of her pussy.

She felt his finger swirl around her pussy lips and up and down her slit. She needed to tell him that she'd never been with anyone before, but she couldn't speak with how he was running his tongue over her clit. It took her ability to speak from her.

When he slowly entered her with one finger, she thought she would explode right then and there. The pressure was unbelievable.

Then he added a second finger, and her world tilted as everything inside of her started to pull back as if waiting for something. He swirled them around inside of her, rubbing over sensitive tissues that took her breath.

"Easy, Destiny. Just relax. Let it happen, darling. Don't fight it." Granger moved his fingers in and out of her pussy until he touched the barrier deep inside of her.

Her startled gasp stilled him. She didn't want him to stop. It felt so good what he and Marty were doing to her. She never wanted it to end.

"Please, Granger. Please don't stop," she begged.

"Never, baby. Hold on. I don't want to hurt you."

She moaned when he covered her clit with his mouth once again. This time he didn't tease her with the tip of his tongue. Instead, he sucked the little bud into his mouth as he stroked over some part of her that felt too good to believe. She felt the pressure build like a latent volcano, ready and eager to explode. The harder he sucked on her clit, the higher her body soared in preparation for a free fall she knew she wasn't ready for.

Granger bit lightly on her clit and rubbed his tongue over the top again and again while he stroked her hot spot with his fingers. Marty bit down and pinched her nipples, sending jolts of pleasure streaking through her body in all directions. Stars exploded behind her eyelids as she squeezed them shut. Her body flew apart into tiny little pieces then came together in a blast that shot her heavenward at the speed of light.

Even long seconds after she'd returned to her body, thrills of pleasure coursed through her bloodstream as Granger continued to lick at her cum, drenching his face. She was much too tired to be embarrassed by what had happened between them, but as soon as she recovered, she wouldn't be able to look at the two men without blushing. She'd screamed and begged like a slut. What would they think of her?

Then she became aware of Marty's hard naked cock bobbing not far from her face as he stretched above her. She looked up at him through her lashes and caught the pained expression on his face. She licked her lips and wondered what it would be like to take him into her mouth. They'd made her feel so good. Shouldn't she return the favor?

Not allowing herself to think too much about it, Destiny reached out and grabbed Marty's thick stalk and squeezed. His startled moan startled her into letting go. At the disappointment etched on his face when she let go, Destiny smiled shyly and wrapped her hand around him once more. When she squeezed, a drop of pre-cum leaked at the slit in the crown. She ran her tongue over it, immediately liking the slightly salty taste.

She licked up and down the thick stalk of Marty's dick, closing her eyes in pleasure as she tasted his musky maleness. Each ridge and bump gave her a new place to explore with her tongue.

"Fuck, Destiny. You're killing me here," Marty said with a groan.

She dragged her tongue all around under the crown, paying close attention to the spot underneath the lip that seemed to be extra sensitive. When he dug his fingers into her scalp, she knew she'd gotten to him. His moans and groans egged her on until she slowly drew in on the mushroom head and closed her mouth around him.

"Fuck! Just like that, honey," Marty hissed out.

She slowly lowered her head down his cock until she hit the back of her throat. She backed off before she gagged, then did it again and again. Each time, she managed to take a little more of him inside of her. His moans and groans along with the subtle kneading of his fingers against her scalp were all the encouragement she needed to continue exploring his stalk with her tongue.

Giving him some of what he'd given her had her flying with him as she took him even deeper into her throat.

"That's it, honey. Swallow around me. Ah! Just like that. So good." Marty's guttural voice tightened her cunt with need once again.

Destiny reached up and caressed his balls with one hand, lightly rolling them in their sac. He tightened his grip on her scalp, digging his nails in slightly. She took that as a positive sign and gently tugged on them before returning to rolling and squeezing the two covered globes.

"Fuck! I'm going to come, honey. Swallow it. All of it, Destiny."

She hummed her agreement and sucked on him harder as his balls drew up in her hand. Spurt after spurt of his cum coated her throat and filled her mouth as she struggled to swallow the salty semen. When he'd finished, she licked him clean then relaxed back against the bed with her eyes closed.

"That was so fucking hot," Granger said with a tight note to his voice.

Destiny realized that she'd left him out of everything, concentrating on Marty. Guilt washed over her, and she started to sit up to reach for Granger, but he shook his head.

"Don't move, darling. I've got plans for you. Do you trust me?" he asked, strain evident in the tightness of his voice.

"I trust you, Granger. What are you going to do?" she asked, unable to hide the uncertainty in her voice.

"I'm going to make you ours, baby. We know you're a virgin. I'm going to be careful, but there will be a little pain at first. You know that, don't you?" he asked.

She nodded, unable to say anything more. She'd expected this since he'd first tried to talk to her the other day. Still, knowing what was to come wasn't the same thing as being ready for it. The books had ranged from making it sound like there was nothing to it to the loss of her virginity being the most painful experience she'd ever have outside of childbirth. All she could do was trust Granger and Marty to take care of her.

"Granger. Maybe we should wait," Marty said.

"No! I don't want to wait. Waiting won't change anything." Destiny wasn't sure where her strength had come from, but she didn't want to wait.

"Easy, darling. Just relax. Let us do all the work." Granger leaned in and kissed her, sharing her taste as he did.

He didn't take or demand from her as she'd expected with his gruffness always so evident. Instead, he coaxed and teased her, giving her the freedom to explore him as Marty had explored her. Desire slowly grew with each tease of his tongue. She whimpered with need, not really knowing what it was she needed.

He slowly pulled away and stared deep into her eyes before licking and nipping at her nipple. Marty joined in on the other one, and pleasure rose fast and sweet inside of her once again. How could it be so good so soon? Destiny moaned and gave herself over to them to take her where they wanted.

* * * *

Granger was wild with need but held back, wanting to be sure she was ready for him. He'd never taken a virgin before, never feeling the need to prove himself or be the first like so many other guys. Instead, he'd treasured the ones who'd lost their innocence in more ways than one, taking pleasure in showing them that it wasn't always disappointing, and there was more to it than a few sweaty minutes in the back seat of some jock's car.

He licked and sucked his way down her body. Each new sensitive spot he found was catalogued to explore later, when they had more time. Right now, he wanted to give her pleasure and take away the pain of her first time. Getting it out of the way so they could all bond and become comfortable with each other was much more important.

Marty took over pleasuring her breasts while Granger returned to her gorgeous pussy. Its pale pink lips grew darker as she became more aroused. He loved seeing them blossom with color, knowing that he was part of the reason. Her clit peeked timidly from beneath its hood, as if remembering there was pleasure to be had but still not sure at the same time. Granger couldn't wait until all they had to do was breathe on her neck or brush against her breasts to elicit desire to bloom in their woman.

"You're so pretty. I could look at your sweet pussy for hours, eat your delicious juices for days," he told her.

Her answering moan tightened his cock. Already rock hard and painful, the pressure of laying on it as he licked and sucked on her cunt was almost more than he could bear, but he wanted to be sure she was ready for him, or as ready as she could be. He wanted to stretch her some so that his intrusion wouldn't be too hard. With cum boiling in his balls, patience wasn't coming easy for him.

He pressed two fingers inside of her, the juices from her recent orgasm giving him plenty of lubrication. He spread them over and over as he pressed in and out of her in shallow thrusts. Her body undulated with him, already attuned to what it wanted from him. He couldn't help but smile in satisfaction that she wanted him.

He pushed slightly deeper with each stroke of his fingers inside her wet cunt. When he encountered the flesh that protected her virginity, he gently pushed at it in time with his sucking on her clit until the slight tightness in her thighs pressed against him relaxed, and she returned to rocking her pelvis in time to his thrusts. Over and over, Granger pushed her until he felt the slight tear of the hymen. He sucked hard on her clit then retreated, leaving her on the edge of orgasm.

When he pulled back and knelt between her legs, his eyes met her wide ones, wild with need. She whimpered and reached for him, an air of desperation surrounding her. He caught Marty's eyes and nodded. The other man kissed her while twisting and tugging on her nipples as Granger plunged into her hot, wet cunt in one deep thrust.

He felt her tear beneath him at the same time she screamed into Marty's mouth, her legs wrapping around Granger's back as if she didn't want him to leave her. He stilled, fighting against the urge to pull out and plunge in again. Her sweet pussy was so tight and wet. He had never felt anything like this before. His cock felt swaddled in a silky, satin clamp that threatened to squeeze him to death. Each ripple of her sensitive tissues around his equally sensitive dick gave new meaning to the word pleasure. Even not moving, he was on the verge of losing it.

"So tight. God, you're so damn tight, Destiny." Granger felt sweat rolling down his face as he fought to remain still, buried deep inside of her.

She tore her mouth from Marty's, pulling his hair to move his head. "Move, damn you! Don't leave me like this!" she screamed.

Granger groaned and pulled back from her perfect embrace. The rasp of her hot cunt over his oversensitive cock was almost more than he could stand. He thrust back inside of her, biting back the need to come. His balls were so tight he expected them to explode at any minute. He refused to let it end this quickly. She would come again before he let go.

Each thrust of his dick into her sweet pussy was sheer torture. The way her body responded as he rasped over her sensitive tissues thrilled him. She had a death grip on Marty's hair as the other man sucked her perfect nipples. Seeing her eyes widen as she watched first Marty, then him, pleasure her only added to the pressure building in his balls.

"Marty, I'm losing it, man. Take care of her," he ground out between clenched teeth.

He struggled not to dig his fingers into her hips as he pounded into her tight cunt over and over, watching as Marty fingered her clit. The surprise on her face when she came again was worth every bit of the torture of holding off a little longer. The ripples of her pussy around his cock squeezed and milked him until he felt fire race down his spine to detonate in his balls.

Nothing could have stopped him from roaring as he shot his cum deep inside of her. He felt it from his curled toes all the way to the tips of his ears. Fuck, he'd have cramps in his ass muscles after this. It felt as if it went on forever. The more she contracted her cunt around his straining dick, the more he came until finally, he collapsed over her.

Marty cursed, pulling out from under him as he caught his weight on his arms to keep from crushing Destiny. All he could do was grunt at the man.

"Hey, asshole. Don't suffocate her. Let her breathe. Roll over." Marty pushed on him until he eased to the side.

Granger slowly pulled free of her still quivering pussy and kissed her neck, burying his nose there while he fought to breathe. He was fucking toast. Nothing had prepared him for her. Her innocence and fearlessness tied him up in knots. Now she was his—theirs. He'd do everything in his power to keep her safe and make her happy.

Marty's gaze caught his over her head. There was a sort of bonding in that look. She'd affected his new friend the same way she'd affected him. He nodded back at the man and closed his eyes to enjoy the moment. Too soon, they would be back on the road looking for a safe place to call home.

Chapter Twelve

Destiny sat in the back seat of the Jeep as they drove toward Broadus on highway two twelve. She watched out the window without really seeing anything. Her mind was too busy reliving that morning to notice the scenery, or lack of it. Everything seemed surreal to her right then. Her body still sang from the orgasms they'd given her, each bump in the road reminding her sore body of how it had sung for them earlier.

"How are you doing back there, ladybug?" Marty asked, watching her through the rearview mirror.

"Good. How much longer 'til we get there?"

"Not long. Maybe another thirty minutes or so. Need anything?" Granger asked, turning to look at her.

"No. I'm fine." She felt heat rush to her skin. All it took was for one of them to smile at her, and she burned all over again.

"She's fucking adorable when she blushes like that," Marty said, glancing back at her.

"Keep your eyes on the road," she fussed.

"Yes, ma'am." Marty just grinned back at her through the mirror again.

She stuck her tongue out at him then giggled like a girl. What was wrong with her?

I'm in love. Not only am I in love with two delicious men, but I had sex with them, and it was freaking amazing!

"What are you thinking about back there, darling?" Granger asked with a knowing smile.

"Nothing."

She refused to look at him. If she did, she'd blush again, and he'd know what she was thinking about. They were enjoying teasing her so that she got all hot and sweaty.

Thirty minutes later, they pulled into the outskirts of Broadus. It looked like a modern day ghost town at first, but as they drove through, evidence that people still lived there could be seen when you looked hard enough. Destiny didn't like the way the place felt, but then she never felt good around populated places.

"We're going to need to get some gas from somewhere," Marty said.

Granger pointed toward a parking lot ahead of them. "Pull in there. We'll check and see if we can siphon any from one of them."

Marty followed his directions and stopped next to an older pickup truck. They sat there for a second looking around, but nothing moved around them.

"Stay inside in case there's trouble. I'll try for the gas." Granger jumped out of the Jeep and pulled a length of hose out from under his seat.

Destiny watched as he walked, opened the gas cap of the truck, and fed the hose into the tank. She looked around, trying to keep watch for anyone that might cause trouble. She heard the gas cap come off of the Jeep next. Still nothing moved around them. Her neck ached from the tension of watching for movement anywhere.

After what seemed like forever, she heard Granger screw the cap back on the Jeep. Seconds later, he opened the Jeep's door and shoved the hose back under the seat. Then he opened a bottle of water and rinsed his mouth.

"Crap, that's nasty. How much does the gas gauge show, Marty? Do we need to find another one?" he asked.

"Looks like a good three quarters full. That should do us for a while. We've got the five gallon can in the back if we get too low," Marty answered.

"Sounds good to me." Granger jumped back into the Jeep.

"Um, guys. Can we find somewhere sort of private? I need to go."
She had tried to wait as long as possible, but since they were stopped
anyway, she didn't think she could wait much longer.

"Gotcha, ladybug. Give me a second to find you somewhere."
Marty pulled out of the parking lot and drove around until he found a
spot behind a store that they could keep watch while she relieved
herself.

They stepped out of the Jeep on one side to take advantage of the
rest stop while she took care of herself on the other side that had the
wall of the store at her back. No one could see her or get to her
without going through them first. As soon as she finished, she cleaned
her hands with the alcohol wipes she'd found and kept in her pack.

When she climbed back in the Jeep, Marty was already inside. He
handed her a bottle of water. The door opened and Granger got in.

"Let's get going. We've been here too long," he said.

Marty started the engine, and they headed back out of town again.
They passed the drive time telling each other a little about themselves.
She listened to Marty talk about how the police department in
Chicago had gone to crap almost immediately. She talked about how
she'd sit and watch people through her binoculars and make up stories
about them to keep her company when she was by herself.

"What about you, Granger? What did you do at first?" she asked.

He glanced over at Marty then stared out the side window in
silence for a few seconds. Finally, he started talking.

"Mostly I just wandered from place to place. I wasn't too upset
about it at the time. I worked for food and a place to sleep just to get
by. Guess you could say I had a bad attitude for a few years.
Eventually that got old, and I decided it was time to settle down in
one place. I knew I didn't want to live in a city or even one of the
smaller towns. People were too paranoid, and most of them would just
as soon shoot you as look at you." He shook his head and didn't say
anything for a few minutes. Destiny could tell he was struggling with

something. She couldn't imagine what would weigh so heavily on him.

"I'd been as far west as Broadview, north of Billings, and liked it out there. The little communities out there are fairly friendly once they know they can trust you. They stick together and help take care of each other. Then I met you and Marty."

"What did you do before everything?" she asked.

"I was an accountant, believe it or not." He sounded bitter about that. Why?

"You sure don't look like an accountant. You don't wear wire-rimmed glasses or have pencils in your pocket," she teased.

"Yeah, well, people change," he said.

After that, the conversation turned to the things they saw along the way. By the time they pulled into Lame Deer, the sun was low on the horizon. Destiny was tired and needed to walk around. Her legs ached from sitting too long. Still, Granger had them drive almost all the way out of the city to the outskirts. He directed them down a gravel road that seemed to lead to nowhere. When they emerged into a gravel parking lot outside what looked like a small town of wooden huts, she saw people freely walking around for the first time since she'd left Atlanta.

"Where are we?" she asked.

"This is a small community of Cheyenne Indians. They're peaceful as long as you don't cause any trouble," Granger told them. "We'll be safe here for the night."

They all got out, and Granger led them to one of the wood buildings where he knocked on the door. As if they'd been waiting for him to knock, the door opened, and a dark-skinned man a little shorter than Granger stepped out and held out his hand.

"Granger. You made your way back to us. Grandmother said you would return," the man said.

"Joe Running Elk, this is my friend, Marty, and our woman, Destiny. This is Joe Running Elk, the chief spokesman of his tribe."

Granger stepped back so that Marty could shake the other man's hand.

"It's great to meet you. Any friend of Granger's is a friend of ours. Do you need a place for the night, my friend?" Joe asked.

"We would appreciate that if you have room. I thought I'd chop some wood for your grandmother while I was here," Granger said.

"She's got plenty for the winter. I could use some help with moving some supplies if you have time." Joe walked out into the front where several children were playing with sticks and a pine cone.

Destiny followed the men, but she kept watching as the children knocked the pine cone around. She'd seen so few children since she'd been living with her aunt and uncle. It made her smile to see them laughing and happy.

"Come on, Destiny. Keep up, ladybug." Marty grabbed her hand and pulled her along with them.

They walked over to another cabin-like building where Joe opened the door. "Here you go. Make yourselves at home."

"Marty and I will be over in a few minutes to help you with those supplies," Granger said.

Joe nodded and left them there. She walked through the door to find that the cabin was a very large, one-room building. The fire place was outfitted for cooking, and the bed was closed on one side for warmth. She noticed that there were only two small windows, one on either side of the room. A couch and a chair sat in front of the fireplace, and a table with four chairs sat on the other side, opposite the bed.

The entire room was clean and smelled fresh despite being empty. They evidently kept it aired out for guests like them. She looked over at Granger and smiled.

"It's cute. It's nice of him to let us use it."

"Marty, let's go get our packs, and then we need to go help Joe's men move supplies for a little while. It's how we're paying for the place to stay tonight. Destiny, stay here. You're safe here, but I'd rather you didn't go anywhere without us." Granger kissed her on top of the head before he and Marty walked back outside to get their packs.

She milled around the room, noticing that the spread on the bed looked handmade. She admired the tiny stitches, wishing she could sew like that. She was decent with a needle and thread, but she couldn't come close to duplicating the needlework. The men walked back in as she was studying the fireplace.

"We'll be gone for a couple of hours. If you get hungry before we get back, go ahead and eat. We can fix ours when we get back," Granger told her.

"I'll be fine. Is it safe enough for me to sit outside while it's still light? I'd like to read some." She held up a book she'd been carrying in her pack.

"No wonder that thing was so freaking heavy," Marty teased. "How many books do you have in that thing?"

"Just one," she said with a grin.

"Don't be surprised if someone comes over to chat. They don't see a lot of people here, especially white people," Granger said. "We'll be back."

Destiny stepped out with them and sat on one of the hand-carved benches sitting in front of the cabin. Sure enough, she soon had several children milling around her, touching her hair and talking among themselves in their tribal language. After a few minutes, a young Indian woman walked up and clucked at the children.

"Sorry if they are bothering you. They are just curious," she said.

Destiny smiled. "They're not bothering me. I love seeing them. I haven't seen many children. Do you want to sit with me?" she asked.

The pretty woman nodded and sat next to her. "My name is Sarah."

"I'm Destiny. This is a very nice place. How many live here?" she asked.

"There are twenty-six of us, including children and our elders. Where are you from?"

"Atlanta, Georgia. I left there almost seven months ago, though. The cities are too dangerous for a woman, and my aunt and uncle whom I was living with were killed in a fire that destroyed our house." Destiny realized that for the first time it didn't feel quite as painful as it once did to think about them.

"I'm sorry for your loss. We've all lost family and friends along the way. Were your parents killed in the great devastation?" Sarah asked.

"Yes. They were killed in one of the tornadoes that came through. That's when I went to live with my aunt and uncle." She watched as the children resumed their stick and pine cone game.

"Are those men you are with yours?" Sarah asked with a shy expression on her face.

Destiny knew by the heat in her cheeks that she was blushing again. "Yes, they are."

"Many men share a woman now, as it is safer for the woman. I have one man, but we live in a close community where we all watch out for each other. Still, he talks about bringing another man to our bed. He says that more people are passing this way, and the dangers are growing." Sarah seemed uneasy as she looked around.

"Has there been trouble here?" Destiny asked.

"Not much. Some, but Grandmother says that bad men are coming soon. We listen to Grandmother. She is our seer, our shaman."

"I hope you are prepared for them and are able to fight them off. Do you know how to fight, Sarah?" Destiny would teach her some moves if she didn't. The idea of someone hurting her or the children there made her ill to think about it.

The other woman smiled. "Oh yes. Joe makes us all practice self-defense constantly. We are all prepared."

"Good. Joe seems like a really nice man and a good leader." Destiny didn't know what to say to the other woman. She wasn't used to making small talk with anyone, having only been around her family and then Granger and Marty.

"Can I ask you something personal?" Sarah finally asked.

"Of course. I'll answer if I can."

The pretty Indian woman studied her hands for a few seconds before speaking again.

"What is it like being with two men at one time?" she finally asked.

"Oh. Um, I'm not sure I can really tell you much. I've only been with Marty and Granger for a few days now. They are very good to me, very careful of me." Destiny wasn't sure what to tell the woman. "Um, it's really good to have two men loving on me at one time. I mean, both of their mouths and, um, hands at the same time and all."

Sarah nodded and shivered as if thinking about it. "I'm scared that I won't be able to take care of two men."

"You shouldn't have to worry about that. They should worry about taking care of you instead. Pleasing you should be more important than their own pleasure." Destiny realized she was quoting from one of the books she'd read back in Atlanta. Maybe real life wasn't actually like that.

"That is what my David says, but I can't help but worry."

"Don't worry, Sarah. They will take care of you, and you will be safer with two men to look after you."

"Perhaps you are right. The other man my David wants to include in our home is his friend. He's a very handsome man like my David, but different, too." Sarah smiled shyly again.

Destiny had a feeling that Sarah was already attracted to her husband's friend but feeling guilty about it. She had so little experience that she didn't feel comfortable telling the other woman it was good if she already liked him. Instead she said nothing, and the other woman changed the subject. They talked for another few minutes before Sarah said she needed to leave and start dinner.

With the sun sinking fast now, she could no longer see to read, so she went back inside and built a fire in the fireplace to fight the evening chill and warm up their meal for a change. She liked it here, but she knew that Granger wanted to go farther west where fewer people lived. It would mean less chance of someone giving them trouble, but it also meant harder living conditions. Destiny sat on the couch and watched the fire, thinking about what the future might hold for the three of them when they finally chose a place to stay.

* * * *

"Grandmother said you would return with your family and stop here for a night. It is good to see you, Granger." Mark, Joe's brother, pulled him in for a quick hug.

"I'm glad to see you up and moving around, Mark." Granger stepped back. "This is my friend, Marty. Marty, this is Mark, Joe's brother."

Marty held out his hand and smiled at the other man. "It's a pleasure to meet you."

"Granger saved my life when a bear attacked me while I was out hunting. I owe him much." Mark lifted his shirt to show the massive scars across his chest and abdomen.

"I was just in the right place at the right time. You'd already killed it, I just shot it so that it didn't land on you when it fell," Granger said.

The other man shook his head with a smile. "Our wife sends her thanks once again. She is in her last days awaiting the birth of our first child."

"Congratulations," Granger said with a smile. "May it be a strong boy to run you ragged, or a pretty princess to give you gray hair."

Mark laughed and slapped him on the shoulder. "I will wish the same for you and your friend. Joe says you have a woman now. You are looking to finally make a home for yourself."

Granger felt his stomach dip at the thought of children. He hadn't really thought that far ahead. By the look on Marty's face, his friend hadn't either. He swallowed down the knot in his throat.

"Thanks, I think."

Joe chuckled. "Come. Let me show you what we need help with."

Granger followed Joe into the large building where they stored their supplies for the tribe. Inside the building, several lanterns had been strategically placed to illuminate the huge eighteen-wheeler trailer that was backed into the other end, ready to be unloaded.

"The men take turns going out and loading supplies from the surrounding towns. Usually two or three men will go and fill up the truck then bring it back here where they unload it and store it. Everyone benefits as they have need," Granger explained to Marty.

"Granger went on many rides with us," Joe said.

"Okay, enough gossiping like old women, guys. Let's get this thing unloaded," Mike said with a chuckle. "I want to get back to my woman."

Granger and Marty worked with the five other men and soon had the trailer emptied and its contents stacked according to type. Mike kept up a steady conversation about what all had occurred since Granger had left about eight months back. Once they had finished and the trailer was swept and closed up for its next trip, Mike left to see about his and Joe's wife while Joe shared a drink of aged whisky with Granger and Marty.

"Grandmother says you won't stay here with us. You will move deeper into the mountains. You're welcome to stay here with your family, Granger. The tribe would take you in," Joe said.

"Thank you, Joe. You pay us a great compliment to offer us a home here with your people, but we need to keep moving," Granger told him.

"I understand. You have a new family waiting for you beyond the Cheyenne nation. Grandmother says your woman will be important to this other family. You need to hurry, though. Winter is close on us. It seems to come sooner each year now."

"What else does Grandmother say?" Granger asked, his chest tight with worry.

He had a healthy respect for Grandmother's predictions. She'd known all about him when he'd never met the woman before. She'd also told him that he would meet the other part of his heart and not recognize her at first. He now knew that had been Destiny, who he'd been attracted to but thought was a boy. No, he didn't take the old woman's words lightly.

"She said that you need to tell your woman what she, Grandmother, already knew about you. It weights heavy on your heart. Trust her with your secrets, Granger." Joe smiled at him. "You know Grandmother. She always talks in riddles."

"But they make sense later," Granger added.

"That they do." Joe stood up and stretched. "Time for us to part for the night. I will see you off in the morning, friend."

Granger nodded, standing as well. "Thanks again for the place to crash."

"Good night, Joe," Marty added as he and Granger walked away from where the other man stood.

"This Grandmother sounds like she knows a lot about you, man. Sounds like good advice to me." Marty's voice held a smile.

"Yeah, I know. I'll talk to her once we get settled. I don't want her to have any reason to doubt me while we're on the road. There's too much at stake." Granger glanced over at the other man.

"I think you're not giving her enough credit. She loves you, Granger. Your past isn't going to change that."

"It might make her hesitate when she doesn't have the time to. I'm not taking the chance with her life." Granger stopped a few steps from the cabin. "I'll tell her, but not now."

Marty shrugged and nodded his head. "I'm not going to say anything. It's your secret to tell. I just think you should go ahead and get it off your chest. I can see it bothering you when you look at her."

Granger pulled his fingers through his hair and shook his head. Without saying another word, he walked up to the door and opened it. He knew Marty was right and he needed to get it out in the open between them, but with all of the dangers ahead of them, he was afraid she might not trust him when her life was in danger. He needed her to follow his directions immediately if things got bad. He'd confide in her as soon as they found a place to stay.

Mike's talk about children hit him again. What would happen if she turned up pregnant before they'd had a chance to make a safe place for her? He hadn't thought once about getting her pregnant. The thought of her round with their baby had his cock hard in seconds. The sight of Destiny's round ass as she bent over the fire stirring something had him groaning as his balls tightened in their sack. Thoughts of abstinence to keep from getting her pregnant flew right out the window.

Chapter Thirteen

"There you two are. I was beginning to think I was going to be eating all alone after all." Destiny smiled as her men walked inside.

"Whatever you're cooking smells delicious," Marty said, pulling her into his arms for a kiss.

The feel of Granger behind her had her nipples hard as diamonds. Both men smothered her with kisses and hugs before easing away. She fanned herself and laughed as both men smiled at her obviously flustered state.

"We're having grilled fish, green beans, and flat bread," she told them. "One of the families sent some fish over that their son had caught today."

"I can't wait," Marty said, sitting down at the table.

"The boy said we should make sure we choose a place that has a river to fish from so we will have fish to eat." She smiled as she served them. "I think he's a very wise nine-year-old. What do you think?"

"I think you're right," Granger said, taking a bite of the fish.

"Mmm, this is delicious, ladybug." Marty flashed her a warm smile.

"Thanks. I wasn't sure if I would remember how to fix them or not. I read about grilling fish, but I'd never actually cooked fish before."

"You could have fooled me," Marty said.

"You taught yourself a lot by reading books, didn't you?" Granger asked.

"Yeah. With everything like it was, there weren't any schools, and it wouldn't have been safe for me to go anyway, so I read everything my aunt and uncle could find to bring home for me." She savored the flavor of the fish she'd seasoned with salt and lemon pepper that was already in the cabin.

"I'm impressed, Destiny. Teaching yourself takes a lot of dedication and self-discipline. Not many teenagers would have stuck with it." Granger's praise pleased her, but it embarrassed her as well.

"Yeah, well. I goofed off a lot, too. I loved reading naughty books. My aunt got them for me. She said that I needed to know what to expect when they found me a good man for a husband. I wonder if she'd read them before she gave them to me. They were pretty wild." She fanned her face just thinking about them.

"Really? What were some of them about?" Marty asked, wagging his eyebrows.

"Never mind. Eat your dinner." She wasn't about to tell them about what she'd read about.

"I'll let you off the hook for now, honey, but after dinner you're going to tell us all about your dirty stories," Marty warned her with a grin.

She glanced over at Granger and saw the way he was looking at her. It had her pussy dripping almost instantly. It was obvious what was on his mind by the way he licked his lips and stared at her with his dark eyes. Her mouth went dry, making it impossible for her to swallow. She gulped the Indian bark tea she'd made and nearly choked.

Marty's chuckle broke the sensual spell Granger had snared her in. She frowned at both men and studiously ignored them as she finished eating. It wasn't right that they could turn her on with just a look. She wanted to affect them like that. Being able to get them hard and horny in an instant would go a long way to getting what she wanted.

Maybe the next time they ventured near a town that had an adult shop, she could talk them into letting her get a few books. After all, they would benefit from them as much as she would. That thought brought a smile to her lips.

"What are you grinning about over there, missy?" Granger asked in a rough voice.

"Nothing. Are you guys finished?" she asked.

Both men stood up and helped her gather the plates. She quickly washed them up in the pan of water Marty brought in for her, and Granger dried them and put them away. She dried her hands on a towel and turned to ask the guys what they wanted to do next and quickly found out when Granger pulled her into his arms for a kiss. His lips pressed tightly to hers before he nipped at her bottom lip and licked across the seam of her mouth.

"I'm thinking it's time we went to bed, darling. We've got a long drive ahead of us tomorrow." Granger laced his fingers with hers and pulled her toward the bed.

Marty had already pulled back the covers and was undressing. Destiny couldn't take her eyes off the other man as he slowly removed his shirt to reveal broad shoulders and a wide chest. The light dusting of hair had her fingers itching to play in it. She wanted to taste his nipples and nip the skin over his tight abdomen.

"God, when you look at me like that I want to holler like Tarzan," Marty said in an amused voice.

"She brings out the beast in both of us," Granger said with a chuckle. "Look at her. She's drooling over you, man."

Destiny felt the blush heat her face as she had to swallow down the saliva that had pooled in her mouth. She couldn't help it that they were so good looking. It was their fault, not hers. Really, they shouldn't tease her like this.

"Now don't pout, ladybug. You're so cute with your tongue sticking out and your eyes wide," Marty said, walking closer to her.

"She has on too many clothes, Marty." Granger pushed her toward the other man.

"I agree. Let's do something about that." Marty began unbuttoning the shirt she was wearing.

Destiny looked back to find Granger pulling his shirt over his head, revealing his hard body to her greedy eyes. She couldn't tear her eyes away from the sight of all that muscle, even when Marty chuckled and pinched her nipple.

"Stop," she fussed, slapping at his hand.

"You're going to get a crick in your neck if you don't stop," Marty teased.

She watched as Granger slowly unsnapped his jeans then lowered the zipper over his massive erection. It sprang out the second the zipper was open. Neither man wore underwear beneath their jeans. She found that odd since they'd worn it to bed with her in the past. She started to ask about that when Granger wrapped his hand around the base of his cock and pumped it slowly, for her benefit she was sure. Her mouth watered once again.

Granger's low chuckle only tightened things low in her belly. Marty unfastened her jeans and after unzipping them, pulled them over her hips and down her legs. Legs that had begun to tremble with anticipation of what was to come.

"Step out, honey." Marty held her hand to help her balance.

Granger had removed his boots and jeans now and was standing before her totally nude, his hand still fisting his thick dick. She wanted to taste him, see what the differences would be between him and Marty.

"Don't worry, darling. I'm going to let you suck my cock in just a few minutes." Granger putting into words what she'd been thinking about had her panting.

"Let's take this to the bed, Destiny. I want you nice and comfortable. It's my turn to taste that sweet honey Granger told me about." Marty helped her on the bed then knelt between her legs. He looked up into her eyes. "I'm going to make you scream, honey. Don't hold back."

Destiny shivered at his words. The idea of needing to scream because it was so good had her halfway there already. But she'd never allow herself to do that with others so close to them. Maybe when they were somewhere away from others she could scream for them. She liked that idea, a lot.

"God, you have the prettiest pussy I've ever seen. I bet it tastes even better than what Granger told me." Marty kissed her above her mound then ran his fingers through her trimmed hair. He tugged on it slightly, sending tingles of pain and excitement straight to her clit.

Granger stretched out beside her, kissing and nuzzling her neck while his fingers played lightly with her nipples. The rasp of his teeth against her shoulder heated her blood. She liked the wildness in him. She wasn't sure where it came from, but it was there, and she knew he was hiding parts of himself from her. She'd uncover them and prove that she accepted all of him. One day, he would tell her.

The first rasp of Marty's tongue up her slit drew a wild moan from her throat even as she lifted her pelvis to follow that playful tongue. He pressed a hand against her belly to hold her still as he teased and licked her pussy lips as if they were pieces of candy. It almost tickled it was such a light touch. She wanted more, though. Destiny didn't want teasing, she wanted temptation too strong for her to resist. She wanted to feel that long hard build they'd given her that morning that ended in an explosion that was almost too much for her to take.

"More, Marty. Stop teasing me. Lick me."

"Listen to her demanding self. You'd think she was the one in charge," Marty said with a soft chuckle.

"You're not in charge, sweet thing. We are. Now settle down and take what we give you." Granger nipped her shoulder harder than before.

"Hey! You're going to leave a mark if you keep doing that," she fussed without really minding.

"That's what I intend to do, mark you so that everyone knows you belong to us. You are ours, Destiny." Granger kissed her, devouring her mouth with his, his hands squeezing and caressing her breasts as he stole her breath.

Marty's tongue slipped between her pussy lips, stabbing inside of her with single-minded determination. Together, they were overwhelming. She didn't stand a chance of holding any form of control over herself. If they wanted her to scream, Destiny knew she would scream.

"You taste like spicy cider. I could drink you down and come back for more." Marty's husky voice had her cunt quivering with need.

They teased and tortured her until she thought she would die if they didn't do something. Her body quivered in expectation, waiting for them to give her what she needed. Then Marty circled her clit with his tongue while exploring her pussy with one finger. It wasn't enough, not nearly enough. She groaned, pushing her pussy closer to his devious mouth. The feel of him chuckling against her delicate parts only amped up the tightness winding inside of her. God, if they ever did let her come she would fly apart.

"Please, Marty. I need to come." She couldn't believe that was her voice begging him. Where had her pride gone?

Granger sucked hard on one nipple, trapping it against the roof of his mouth as he teased it with his tongue. The other one he pulled and twisted with his fingers, giving her just enough pain to heighten the pleasure she knew was to come. He released the nipple he held in his mouth to suck in as much of her breast as he could. Always, he was careful of her shoulder, never putting pressure on it or pulling that breast more than he thought was safe. How could a man so considerate of her be hiding something so terrible inside that he didn't want her to know about it? She couldn't accept it.

Marty entered her with two fingers now, stretching and filling her as he lapped at her juices that poured for him. Oh, God, she needed more. She wanted him to fill her with his cock and fuck her like Granger had early that morning. When had she become so wanton? Just minutes before she'd been too embarrassed to scream so that others could hear her. Now she wanted them to hear how good her men made her feel.

Without warning, Marty sucked her clit into his mouth and grasped the tiny ball of pleasure with his teeth. He rasped his tongue over it again and again as he stroked his fingers over her sweet spot with surprising accuracy. Together with Granger's attention to her nipples, it completely devastated her. She did scream until Granger abandoned her breasts to take her scream into his mouth.

Destiny dug her nails into Granger's shoulders when she couldn't reach Marty's head. She had to have something to hold onto. There was no way she'd be able to remain grounded without it. Her body disintegrated around her soul, even as her heart melted in the heat of her orgasm. The books had never described it this way. Had the authors never really come before? God, it was almost painful it was so good.

She fought to breathe around the tightness in her chest that reminded her how much she loved them. It demanded she tell them, but Destiny held back. She wanted all of them before she gave all of herself. Granger was holding back, so she would, too.

Even as she began to ease back from the intense pleasure that filled her body, Marty had pulled away from her pussy and was saying something to Granger. In one smooth flip, she found herself on her hands and knees with Granger's cock bobbing in front of her. Yes! She stuck out her tongue and licked the spongy fat crown and grinned at his sharp hiss of breath.

Chapter Fourteen

Marty stared at the perfect picture before him. Destiny on her hands and knees with her delicious ass in the air and her legs spread wide. He couldn't wait to sink into her sweet cunt, feel her hot, wet tissue surround his aching cock. Never had he wanted inside of a woman as badly as he wanted to be inside of this woman, their woman.

He caressed her rounded globes as he realized he was slowly coming to accept that he was sharing her with a man he still barely knew. Accepting that it was the best way to keep her safe was far easier than he thought it should have been. He squeezed her ass then spread her cheeks so that her pussy gaped before him and the tiny star of her back hole winked at him. They hadn't talked to her about anal sex yet, but he and Granger had discussed it. Granger seemed to know a lot about it while Marty had only heard others talk about it. He wasn't sure how he felt about it.

"Marty!" Destiny moaned, wiggling her ass. "Please, fuck me."

He groaned at the sound of her husky voice begging him to fill her with his cock. He fit the tip of him at her entrance and slowly fed it to her, one throbbing inch at a time. She tried to back into him and take him faster, but he held her still, his fingers digging into her heavenly cheeks.

Granger had suggested that he play with her back hole some to start preparing her so they didn't hurt her. While he wasn't sure it was something he really wanted to do, he knew Granger did and was going to be sure their woman was prepared. He couldn't stand the idea of causing her pain. He'd no doubt fight Granger over it if he dared hurt her. Deep inside, though, Marty was sure Granger would never knowingly do so.

He pushed his swollen dick deeper into her hot, wet cunt and closed his eyes at the ecstasy. She was so tight, so wet and tight. He felt as if he were shoving his stiff cock into a velvet glove, fresh from a hot dryer. This was like nothing he'd ever felt before. He'd just thought her mouth was heaven.

"Fuck, that's it, darling. Suck my cock." Granger's head was thrown back as their woman wrapped her mouth around his friend's dick. The sight of her lips stretched tight around the other man's penis made his balls ache.

"Her cunt is like sinking into a vat of warm molasses, man," Marty said.

"I can't believe you're comparing me to food." Destiny had pulled off of Granger's dick and turned to frown at him over her shoulder.

Granger grabbed her hair and pulled her back around. "Stop complaining and swallow me down, Destiny. I want to feel your throat around my dick."

Marty chuckled at the scowl she gave the other man before she did just that and took him to the back of her throat. He could tell by the way Granger's face twisted into painful pleasure that she was giving him her best. His mouth opened, and he groaned low in his throat.

"Just like that. Aw, fuck, your mouth is made of sin, darling." Granger's voice had gotten so deep it almost hurt Marty to listen to it.

Marty looked down at where his cock was halfway inside of her sweet putty and sank all the way inside of her until he felt the tip of him touch her cervix. Her moan and the way she wiggled her butt let him know it felt good to her. Some women didn't like the bite of pain hitting their cervix caused, but she obviously did. He relaxed and pulled out, glad that he could go all the way inside of her without worrying about hurting her. He wasn't huge, but he was long enough that he usually bottomed out in most women.

He reveled in the pleasure of thrusting back inside of her tight pussy. Her hot tissues sucked at him each time he pulled out, as if begging him not to leave her. He pounded into her over and over, his shaft growing harder with each slide inside of her. He reached beneath her and gathered her cream to coat her back hole in it. She tensed beneath him, but Granger saw what he was doing and held her still.

"He's just playing with you, darling. Relax, and let him open you some back there. You know we're going to want to take you together one day, baby. It'll feel so good to have both of us inside you at the same time," Granger's voice crooned to her, even as he appeared to fight the need to come.

Marty circled her tight asshole with the tip of one finger. Slowly, she relaxed around him, letting him know she was trying. He dipped his finger into her little rosette, surprised at how hot she was there, even hotter than her sweet cunt. He added more of her juices to the mix and pressed deeper into her little hole. When he'd managed to work his finger most of the way in, he slowly moved it in and out as he pumped her pussy with his cock. The eroticism of it nearly overwhelmed him. He hadn't expected to like this, but feeling her hot ass tight around his finger was making his balls ache.

Marty looked up to see Granger's knowing smile tight with need as Destiny sucked the man's cock, bobbing up and down his shaft. Granger held up two fingers and dropped his gaze to where Marty's finger was buried in Destiny's back hole. The thought of adding another finger both scared him and turned him on more than he was comfortable with.

When he added the second finger, pressing past the tight ring that guarded her back entrance, he heard her moan around Granger's cock. The way she wiggled her butt told him she was fine with it. He relaxed and slowly moved his fingers in and out as he fucked her, gripping her hip with his other hand. The way she accepted them, eager for more, amazed him. She had been through so much, and here she was taking on two men and all they were offering her.

"Hell, yes, baby! That's it. Swallow around me. Oh, fuck! I'm going to come." Granger's roar of release pushed him closer to his as Destiny tightened around him.

Marty's balls were so fucking tight he didn't know how much longer he could hold off. He wanted it to last, wanted to stay buried deep inside her forever. He continued to spread her virginal hole with his fingers as he pumped in and out of her tight pussy. The sight of Destiny's swollen lips as she looked back at him was the last straw. He groaned as she licked those ruby red lips and pushed back against his thrusts. Fire, hot and sharp, settled in his balls, and boiling cum erupted from his cock deep into her waiting cunt.

He was barely aware of her shout as she tightened around him even more, her own release on the heels of his. Her body quivered around him, milking his dick with each spasm of her tight cunt.

He felt as if he'd never stop coming as he held his cock deep inside her. He leaned over her, his sweaty chest rubbing against her equally wet back. He bit her shoulder to stop from saying something he wasn't ready to admit out loud. The words were on the tip of his tongue to tell her he loved her, but he held back. It was all too new, too raw inside of him.

Instead, he placed soft kisses down her back and gently pulled from her body before rolling over to his back to try and settle himself. His heart raced even as his lungs fought to draw in enough air. The feel of her settling her head on his chest over his galloping heart eased a bit of the nervousness he felt at having not told her that he loved her. It was as if she already knew and was waiting on him to tell her.

Marty closed his hand over her shoulder as Granger settled against her back. The weight of his friend pressed their woman closer to him. She curled her hand under his chin and sighed.

"Goodnight, guys."

"Night, ladybug," he told her softly.

Granger grunted behind her, but she giggled, telling Marty that the other man had told her in his own way. Closing his eyes, Marty prayed that the next day would end the same way, with her between them after making love.

* * * *

At some point in the night or early morning hours, Granger woke her with his cock pressing into her pussy from behind. She smiled, liking that the man needed her again so soon after she'd taken him in her mouth. She moaned seductively and pressed back against his thick dick.

"Go back to sleep, baby. I didn't mean to wake you. I just needed inside of you again." Granger's rough voice had an almost desperate sound to it.

Destiny turned her head to look back at him, but Granger buried his face in her neck and groaned as he buried his cock all the way inside of her. It took her breath to be stretched by him so deliciously. She couldn't help but moan. She tightened her pelvic muscles, knowing it would make it all the better for him. Sure enough, he cursed quietly under his breath as he pulled back then pumped inside of her once again.

"Fuck, I can't get enough of you. Don't ever leave me, Destiny. Nothing can happen to you. You've got to do what we say so we can keep you safe."

His words sounded desperate, as if he was sure he would lose her somehow. It tightened the hold he already had on her heart. That he had such deep feelings for her thrilled her. Still, she wanted to know what he was holding back when he obviously wasn't holding back the way he felt about her. He might not have said the words, but she knew they were there, waiting to come out. She could wait on them. She could wait on his secret—for a while.

There was no urgent need now as he slowly pierced her body with his hard shaft. The almost gentle rocking was soothing as much as it was arousing. He filled her to the point of pain, yet it was so good, so very good. She hummed with the almost magical quality of his possession of her. She couldn't believe that Marty was sleeping through the motion of Granger's thrusts, despite how smooth they were.

"You feel so good inside of me, Granger. I love the way you fill me up," she whispered.

"Play with your clit, baby. Make yourself come for me. I want your cunt to squeeze the cum from my cock," he whispered back next to her ear.

She hesitated to touch herself with him right there. She'd rarely done it alone when living with her aunt and uncle, too shy to actually do it with them in the next room.

"Please, baby." He reached around her and took her fingers into his hand. "Just rub that sweet pearl for me, Destiny."

She let him position her finger over her clit and move it in a circle around it. Immediately, need built inside of her. She couldn't stop the slight gasp of surprise that she'd actually get turned on with him knowing what she was doing.

"See, baby. It's all good. You can play with yourself. Do it for me." His hot breath in her ear and then against her neck as he groaned with each slide of his dick into her wet pussy sent chills down her spine.

Destiny slowly took over playing with her clit. She circled the tight bud over and over before tapping it lightly and then starting over. A warm buzz built as she masturbated with Granger knowing what she was doing. She reached back and felt his hard cock where it separated her pussy lips as it tunneled into her cunt. At the touch of her fingers on his shaft, Granger groaned low and guttural in her ear.

She rubbed up and down it, then returned to playing with herself, ramping up her pleasure with each stroke of her finger. Her body seemed to shine with the wonderful feelings pouring through her right then. This orgasm was going to be so different than the others she'd had. It wasn't a huge build up that would tear her apart then re-make her. It would be a gentle burst of ecstasy that might be even more devastating than the others.

Her breathing grew faster the closer she moved toward climax. Her body tightened all over, making Granger's thick dick even more enormous inside her pussy. She gasped as it slowly rolled over her, consuming her with pleasure and an unbelievable satisfaction as her spasms pulled Granger along with her. He grasped her shoulder with his teeth and groaned low and long as he pulsed inside of her, his seed filling her with scalding heat.

When he released her shoulder, Granger kissed her tender flesh and pulled her against him, still buried inside of her. She nearly laughed out loud when he almost instantly started snoring. It was so funny, yet it filled her with a deep sense of joy to know that she had been what he had needed to relax and rest. She liked that she could do that for him. He stayed so on edge all the time, worrying about the dangers out there.

Destiny held on to the hand that he'd wrapped around her waist. She felt safe there in his arms with Marty at her front. Between them, nothing could get to her. They would protect her with their lives. She knew this but prayed that it would never come to that. Losing even one of them would kill something inside of her.

Granger's flaccid cock slowly slipped from her body. She mourned the loss, feeling so much closer to him while it had been cocooned inside of her. She desperately wanted him to confide in her whatever it was that he still held back. Part of her wanted to confront him and demand that he tell her what was wrong, but another part of her sensed that she needed to wait and let him tell her in his own time. Neither part of her approved of the small empty spot that was still waiting to be filled by that piece of him.

When she finally closed her eyes and pushed the worry and unease back, Destiny fell asleep, dreaming of a place where they had a home and others around them who were friends. She felt safe there and happy. Both of her men were always close by, and the sounds of children playing lightened the deep seated fear that the world would never again be a place where children could run and laugh without being afraid.

Chapter Fifteen

As they left Joe and Mike's Cheyenne Indian tribe behind them, Destiny began to feel a little lonely. She'd enjoyed the conversation with Sarah and watching the children play. Many of the residents of the camp had come out to see them off despite how early it had been. They'd sent them off with gifts of jerky, fresh water from the creek, and a case of different canned vegetables.

Now, as they headed toward Busby, Destiny thought about her dream of the night before and how normal it had felt at the time. Thinking back about it, she recognized that she'd still had to warm up their meals over a fire and there was no electricity, but she'd been happy and satisfied, content even.

"What are you thinking about back there, ladybug?" Marty asked, turning around to stare at her.

"Just wondering where we'll end up, and what we'll do to get ready for winter. We won't have much time. It's already growing cold at night."

Granger looked at her through the rearview mirror. "Don't worry about it, Destiny. We'll take care of you."

She rolled her eyes and pointed toward the road. "You keep your eyes on the road. I know you'll take care of me, but it doesn't change things. We're going to have to be careful of our food supply until we get a garden in the ground and it starts producing."

"Marty and I will keep fresh meat on the table for us. We'll be fine." Granger's hands tightened on the steering wheel.

She could see the way his knuckles grew white with the pressure. She wished she hadn't brought it up now. He didn't need to worry about something that hadn't happened yet. They had enough to worry about.

"Have either of you been to Busby before? How big is it?" she asked.

"I've been through it once," Granger said. "It's smaller than Lame Deer was. I remember seeing somewhere that they had a population of about eight hundred before the disasters. Now, I don't know. There were still people there when I was there almost a year ago."

"Are you planning to stop anywhere?" she asked.

"Not unless you need to pee," he said with a smirk.

She frowned at him. "I don't. I was just curious. If we go anywhere that has a bookstore, I'd really like to grab a few books."

Both men laughed and shook their heads. She crossed her arms and glared at the back of their heads.

"What is so damn funny? It wouldn't hurt for us to have a few books on gardening and caning and such." She wasn't about to admit that she wanted to look for some erotic romances as well.

"Nothing, darling. We'll watch for bookstores for you. You're right. We'll need all the help we can get on things like that." Granger's soothing words somehow didn't sound as sincere as he probably thought they would.

An hour later, they drove through Busby without seeing a soul. Granger said there were still people there, but Destiny would have to take his word on that. She couldn't tell by the way the place looked. The buildings all looked empty to her, and there was debris all over the sidewalks and streets. If she'd been living there, she would have wanted to clean the place up. When she said as much out loud, Marty explained that it was safer for the place to look deserted.

"That way anyone intent on causing trouble will assume no one lives there and continue on without stopping to investigate."

"They've probably learned the hard way through past mistakes," Granger added.

"It's so sad that we have to live in fear," she said, gazing out the window as they left the little town behind.

No one spoke for a long time. At some point, Destiny must have dozed off, because she jerked awake when they ran over a bump.

"What? Where are we?" She looked around confused.

"We're at Crow Agency, the center of the Crow Indian Reservation. There's a bookstore here, if it looks safe enough," Granger said as they drove down a bumpy road.

He turned down one street after another before pulling up next to an old truck outside a book store. He and Marty exchanged glances, then Marty got out and pulled out the hose they used to syphon gas.

"Okay, sit tight while I check the store to be sure it's safe inside. Don't unlock the door unless either me or Marty tell you to. Got it?" Granger asked.

"Okay. Be careful, Granger." She wasn't sure she wanted him to take the risk of checking out the store now.

She watched as he pushed the door lock then closed the door. He and Marty exchanged a few words, then Granger walked up to the building housing the book store. He looked through the window then tried the door. It didn't budge. He disappeared around the side of the building where she could no longer see him. Her heart began to beat faster. She looked over where Marty was standing with one end of the hose in the truck's gas tank and the other one disappearing into the Jeep. He looked around, keeping watch.

After nearly ten minutes, Granger walked out the front entrance of the bookstore with a smile. Destiny almost passed out with relief. He and Marty talked while Marty finished up with the gas, then he motioned for her to unlock the door.

"Okay, you have twenty minutes to find some books, then we need to get back on the road. I don't like sticking around these places too long," Granger told her as they walked into the store.

She was thankful for the lantern he'd lit for her since there was very little light in the building. Only two windows in front and one on the side allowed sunlight inside. Destiny quickly located the right section for gardening and, after picking out a few books from there, found a section on survivalism that contained books on putting up food. She grabbed several books from that section, thinking they might come in handy later.

After dumping these where Marty kept watch at the front, she hurried over to the romance section and quickly located the erotic romance books. She chose the ones concerning ménages since she was now living in one. She also chose a couple of paranormal shape shifting books since she loved that genre. She'd just returned to where Marty waited when Granger walked up with quite a few books of his own. She lifted an eyebrow at the sight and got a sheepish smile from him.

"I figured you were right, and we could use as much help as we could get. These may come in handy," he said.

She refrained from crowing over him agreeing with her about the books. Some things were better left alone. She just grinned to herself and nodded to Marty, looking pointedly at her pile of books at his feet.

Marty shook his head and picked up the books. The three of them walked outside toward the Jeep, talking about the next leg of their journey. Destiny waited while Granger and Marty piled the books in the back seat. When Granger turned to help her into the back, icy cold dread seeped into her pores at the sound of a nasty-sounding cough at her back, close enough she felt hot breath against her neck. Hard fingers bit into her shoulder from behind.

"Well, well, Granger. Fancy seeing you here after all these years. Aren't you going to introduce me to your friends?" a harsh voice asked.

"Calhoun. Take your hand off of her. Now." Granger's voice remained calm but firm.

"Now is that anyway to talk to an old friend?" the other man asked, making a tsking noise.

"We've never been friends, Calhoun. Let her go."

Destiny watched Marty step slowly closer to Granger. He had his hand loose out to his side. She knew he was wearing a gun at the small of his back. She prayed he didn't have to use it. If he did, things would be much worse than she hoped they were. Still, the way the man's fingers dug into her sore shoulder wasn't very comforting.

"Considering what all we went through together, I'd think you would be more considerate than this. I mean, we bonded and all in prison all those years. Remember?"

Destiny tried not to let her face show the shock she felt at hearing that he had been in prison before. Why hadn't he told her before now? She realized this was the part of himself he'd kept from her. She wanted to ask why he'd been there, but she wasn't about to say anything with some stranger standing there with his fingers digging into her.

"There was no bonding, Calhoun. There was no anything between us. Now let her go before you regret it." Granger's voice had dropped even deeper.

"I'm hurt. After what we shared? I'd think you would be a little nicer to me, bitch."

Destiny watched Granger's jaw tighten and the scar on the side of his face grow white from the strain. His eyes changed to cold hard orbs that didn't show an ounce of humanity in them. He took a step closer and the man holding her jerked her against his chest. The scent of unwashed flesh was cloying now that she was pressed tightly against him. She couldn't see how things could get much worse, but she was wrong.

The unmistakable ridge of hard, aroused flesh pressed against her ass. The bastard wanted her. Fear chilled her blood. Her legs began to shake. She should never have stopped dressing like a boy. How was she going to get away from this man?

She tried to focus on Marty. She couldn't look at Granger right then with the way his face had turned into a cold mask. Marty seemed to be trying to tell her something, but she couldn't figure out what it was. His eyes kept looking down at her feet. Destiny got an idea and started struggling with the man, catching him by surprise.

"Be still, or I'll cut you." He pulled out a knife from somewhere. The sight of the wicked-looking blade already stained with something that looked a lot like dried blood made her stop struggling.

He chuckled and nodded toward Marty. "Don't get any ideas, or I'll carve her up like a tasty roast. Got it?"

"I'm warning you, Calhoun. If you harm one hair on her head, I'll gut you. Do you hear me?" Granger's voice still hadn't grown any louder.

"Ah, is she your woman, Granger? Are you and your friend over there sharing her? Do you remember how they held you down while I fucked you back in prison, Granger? Did it feel good?"

Destiny couldn't stand hearing how Granger had been raped, nor could she stand to see the flash of pain that crossed his face before the cold mask snapped back into place. She screamed and rammed her head back as hard as she could, feeling the sharp knock to her skull from his chin. She let herself go limp as if it had knocked her out, and when he didn't react in time to stop her from slipping from his grasp, she shoved her body away from his.

The sound of flesh hitting flesh snapped her head up in time to see Granger plow his fist into the other man's face. The bastard howled with fury. Marty grabbed her and pulled her into his arms, then shoved her into the still-open door of the Jeep and slammed the door.

When she looked up again, Granger and the other man were struggling over the knife. Marty had his gun out and was trying to get a clear shot. She watched as Calhoun managed to get the knife close to Granger's throat. She covered her mouth, afraid she'd make some noise that would distract Granger and get him killed.

They struggled back and forth, neither man getting the upper hand until Calhoun stumbled in a hole in the sidewalk and Granger was able to shove the knife toward the other man. It buried to the hilt in the man's throat. Destiny turned her head away at the sight of blood pouring from the man's throat.

She heard Marty yelling at Granger to get in the Jeep. Then the doors opened, and both men climbed in on opposite sides, slamming the doors behind them. Marty started the engine and shoved it into gear. No one said a word as they hurtled through town, the only sounds the two men's heavy breathing. She fought to keep from getting sick. She refused to throw up. The man would have raped and maybe even killed her.

"Are you okay, Destiny? Did you get cut anywhere?" Marty's voice sounded fairly normal considering they'd just killed a man.

"No, I mean, yes. I'm okay. I didn't get cut." She was shaking so hard she was surprised she was able to speak at all.

"I'm sorry, Destiny." Granger's words sounded almost torn from him.

"Why? It wasn't your fault. You didn't make him grab me," she said.

"He might have hurt you. I should have kept you safe."

"Shut the fuck up, Granger. You did keep her safe." Marty seemed to know what was going on. Destiny was still confused.

"Granger, you couldn't have known he was there. It's not your fault. It's over now, anyway. I'm fine." She wanted to climb into the front seat and curl up in his lap, but he had blood all over him. She didn't want that bastard's blood on her, and she wanted it off of Granger as well.

"We need to find somewhere you can change clothes and get cleaned up," Marty said, echoing her thoughts.

"Pryor is not far ahead. Stay on this road," Granger finally said in a hollow voice.

"Not much of a road," Marty commented.

Destiny ached inside for Granger. Not only did he feel like he had failed her, but his deepest darkest secret had been callously revealed by his enemy. His being in prison was what he'd held back from her.

She doubted he would have ever revealed to anyone that he'd been raped while there, more than likely he'd shut that part off from himself as well. Now he couldn't pretend it had never happened since they'd heard it. Did he think she wouldn't want him anymore? She would make sure he knew that wasn't true as soon as they stopped and he got cleaned up.

* * * *

Granger quickly tore the bloody shirt off his body and tossed it to the side. Anger, red hot and dark, boiled inside of him. He'd been stupid to think he could have someone as sweet and innocent as Destiny. She sure as hell didn't deserve a bastard like him. It didn't matter that he'd been innocent of the charges that landed him there. He was still an ex-con. One who'd been violated by the son of a bitch he'd just killed.

He looked down at the blood stains on his hands and fought down the nausea. He'd killed a man with his hands. He'd beat the hell out of men in the past when it needed doing, and shot and killed those who'd tried to kill them back when they'd first been on the run, but he'd never taken a life before with his hands and been happy doing it. He'd derived a small amount of pleasure feeling the knife dig into Calhoun's throat, and that was what sickened him the most. Only a monster took pleasure in killing someone.

He spat out a curse and quickly washed up, scrubbing his skin raw with the soap, using the jugs of distilled water they'd found in the little grocery they'd stopped at. When he was satisfied that there wasn't any blood on him anywhere, he quickly dressed, leaving the bloody clothes on the floor in the bathroom and returned to the front of the store. Before he knew what hit him, Destiny threw herself into his arms, wrapping her arms around him so tightly he had to fight to breathe.

"God, I was so scared, Granger. I thought he would hurt you. I couldn't bear it if anything happened to you or Marty."

"Ease up, Destiny. I can't breathe." Something inside of him loosened to the feel of her arms around him.

She relaxed her grip slightly but still held on. He tried to pull her back from him, but she wouldn't let go.

"I love you, Granger. Please don't leave me." He froze because that was exactly what he'd been thinking of doing.

"He's not going anywhere, ladybug." Marty pressed against her back and stared hard into Granger's eyes. "Are you, Granger?"

He didn't say anything for a few seconds, trying to swallow around the lump in his throat at the acceptance he saw in the other man's eyes. He felt Destiny stiffen between them at his hesitation.

"No. I'm not going anywhere." He cupped her cheeks in his hand and drew her face up to look at him. "I love you, darling. I won't leave you, ever."

The relief and love in her eyes nearly undid him. He had to swallow again to keep from choking up. He kissed her gently on the lips, then hugged her back.

"I suggest we get back on the road and find a safe place to stay for the night," Marty said.

"Good idea. Come on, woman. I want you to read one of those dirty little books you think you snuck in on us." Granger stepped back and smiled down into her shocked face. "Did you really think I wouldn't have noticed what you were carrying?"

"I'm not reading out loud where you two can hear me." Destiny's outrage was so damn cute.

"Yes, you are. Marty wants to hear all about how three people make love at the same time. Don't you, man."

"I sure do. I can't wait to hear you say all of those dirty words out loud, ladybug. I bet there's a naughty woman inside of you just waiting to come out." Marty popped her on the ass as they headed for the door.

Granger felt lighter than he'd felt in years. All the tightness from keeping what had happened back in prison his dark secret was gone. The fear that Destiny would leave him when she found out he'd been in prison had been for nothing. He felt free, freer than he'd been despite his release from prison years ago.

It hit him that she hadn't even asked about why he'd gone to prison in the first place. He loved her for that alone, but he wanted her to know that he hadn't been a murderer or thief. She deserved the truth of what had happened to him. He needed to tell her.

As soon as they were settled back in the Jeep, he gave her a little respite from having to read to them from her naughty books and told them about how he'd ended up going to jail in the first place. He gave them all the sordid details of how his best friend and fiancé had used and betrayed him. When he was finished, the last of the chains that had held him back and buried that fun loving man he'd once been crumbled into rust.

Chapter Sixteen

"I can't believe you made me read that out loud!" Destiny was so glad she was sitting in the back seat where they couldn't stare at her while she'd read. She was even more thankful that the sun was beginning to set so she couldn't see well enough to read any longer. She was sure that her face and neck were beet red. She was hot enough with embarrassment to blow smoke. Not to mention she was hornier than the devil himself.

"You're so cute when you're red and flustered," Marty told her.

"It was funny how when she got to the sex parts her voice got so soft we had to make her repeat what she'd said," Granger teased, glancing at her through the rear view mirror.

"Stop already, you two. No more. I need to catch my breath and cool off." Destiny fanned herself.

"Oh, boy. Our woman is all fired up. Can't wait 'til we find somewhere to spend the night," Marty said.

"If you don't behave, you'll go without."

"Somehow I can't see you depriving yourself of a little pleasure, darling," Granger said with a smirk.

Damn him, but he was right. She was so turned on and hot right now she wasn't sure she could be still. All she could think about was having both of them inside of her at the same time now. Her panties were soaked, and her nipples so sensitive that the draw of her shirt across them was sheer torture.

"Just find somewhere for us to spend the night. I'm tired." She knew she sounded petulant, but she didn't care at the moment. She felt petulant.

Their soft chuckles only made her madder. Mostly she was mad at herself for being so needy. She was a grown woman. She shouldn't get this hot and bothered just reading a book. She hadn't remembered getting this way before. Of course, before she'd been a virgin and hadn't known what the real thing was actually like. She sighed and dropped her head back against the seat.

They'd been driving for hours and hadn't found anywhere that looked safe enough to stop for the night. They were going to end up sleeping in the Jeep if they didn't find something soon. The fading light wasn't conducive to searching a place to be sure it was safe.

"This looks like a good place to check out," Granger said, pointing over to an old gas station that looked older than dirt.

She leaned forward as they parked under the canopy. The faded sign had said Dave's Stop and Shop. She wondered what had happened to Dave and if anyone was inside waiting on them.

"We all go inside together," Granger said, climbing out of the Jeep. "I don't want to be separated with it being so close to dark."

Once they were all three standing at the door to the building, Granger banged on it just in case someone was actually living there. The sound echoed around them in the encroaching night. No one answered, and no sound could be heard from within. She wasn't sure whether to feel relieved or not. She carried the lantern since Granger needed both hands for his rifle and Marty had both of his revolvers out.

"Looks like we have the place to ourselves, guys." Marty tested the door and found it unlocked.

He and Granger exchanged glances. They both repositioned their weapons in their hands.

"Stay between us, baby. Don't wander off." Granger squeezed her arm then led the way into the store.

The shelves inside had been picked clean. There wasn't much of anything left. The shadows created by the lantern looked creepy as they walked between the shelves to the back of the store. Though musty smelling, it didn't have the smell of death or decay. Evidently, anything perishable had been removed long before it started to rot.

"Clear up here. Let's check the back," Marty said.

They filed through the door leading to the back, where a small storage and office area could be seen. Again, there wasn't much of anything left to pick through, but it was fairly clean and had enough room they could spread out their blankets to sleep.

"Looks good. What do you think, Granger?" Marty studied the door and the locks on it.

"It will do. Let's get what we need out of the Jeep and lock everything down." Marty pushed the rolling chair closer to the door. "Have a seat, Destiny. You're going to stay here while we grab what we need. It's going to be dark since we'll need the lantern, but you're safe."

She sat down and relinquished the lantern to Marty reluctantly. She didn't like sitting in the dark no matter how short a time period it would be. She had spent far too many nights all alone in the dark wondering what or who would find her. It took all of her concentration to remain sitting in the chair waiting on the men to return.

Twenty minutes later, they had the bedding on the floor and a meal of sorts set up. Relief to be locked safely inside the back room helped to settle her stomach enough to eat. They discussed how much farther they might have to go before they found a place to stay. Destiny remained quiet, just listening to them. She could feel the tension beginning to settle over them with the cooler air. Winter would be there soon, and they hadn't found a safe place to live.

"What is it, ladybug?" Marty asked, pulling her into his arms. "You've been awfully quiet."

"Just tired, I guess." She wasn't about to voice what they were all thinking.

"Let's get some sleep." Granger had already removed his boots. Now he unfastened his jeans and stepped out of them.

Instantly, her mouth went dry at the sight of his erection tenting the front of his boxer briefs. She wasn't sure she'd ever seen him not aroused. It was as if his cock remained hard all the time.

Marty's soft chuckle next to her told her he'd noticed where her eyes had been. She felt her face heat. They were always embarrassing her. She didn't think they did it on purpose, but she was easy to tease.

"Granger, she's eyeing you like a hungry wolf watching a rabbit. I think you're the rabbit." Marty comparing Granger to a rabbit was almost silly.

"I think you've got it all wrong, Marty. I'm the wolf about to devour a little rabbit with one bite." Granger stalked over to where Destiny sat next to Marty.

He stood in front of her, his hard cock inches from her mouth. She couldn't stop herself from smoothing her hand over the material and grabbing the stalk through it. He hissed out a breath then pulled her to her feet. Destiny didn't let go of the hold she had on his dick, squeezing and rubbing up and down the length of him.

"Marty, get undressed and lay back on the covers. Destiny here is going to ride you. Aren't you, baby?"

She knew what was coming. It was right out of the book she'd been reading to them. A sharp thrill arced through her body that they were both going to take her together. Finally. She wanted this, but at the same time, she was scared. It wasn't the pain that had her hesitating. She knew there would be some, and that didn't bother her so much. It was the intimacy of the act, the implications that went along with it.

Destiny already thought of herself as belonging to them, but this seemed to be so much more serious and permanent. Allowing them to take her together gave them absolute control over her body. She'd be helpless between them, counting on them to take care of her. Why it was any different than before, she didn't know, but it was.

When Marty finished undressing, he lay back on the bedding they'd laid out and smiled up at her. His eyes were dark with desire, his cock hard and long, the crown lying at his belly button. He lifted his arms to her, sending a silent thrill through her bloodstream that he wanted her and waited on her.

Without letting herself think any further, Destiny let him help her to her knees, straddling him. She leaned over and kissed him lightly on the lips, the touch of his firm lips giving her a little more courage to pursue what she wanted without overanalyzing it. He smiled in the shadowy light of the lantern and gave her a wink. It went a long way to calming her tattered nerves. He always seemed to know how to help her relax. She loved him for that, loved that he understood and wanted to comfort her.

She reached between them and grasped his rigid dick, guiding her body over the fat mushroom head. Already, her pussy was slick with her juices in anticipation of being filled. She rubbed him back and forth over her slit, wetting the crown. His groans at her teasing gave her the confidence to slowly sink an inch onto him before pulling back off and teasing them both some more.

"Stop screwing around, honey. Take me all." Marty's thick voice told her he was fighting the need to thrust up into her cunt.

She laughed, the sound coming out throaty and sexy even to her ears. She relaxed her muscles and allowed her body to slowly slide down his hard cock. As each inch of his shaft filled her body, she moaned. The wiry hair surrounding his dick mingled with hers as she rested flush against his pelvis. She swore she could feel him in her throat.

"Fuck, that's good." The words seemed to be torn from Marty's throat.

Destiny squeezed around him, thrilling at his guttural moan. His fingers dug into her hips as he pushed upward, trying to get even deeper when there was nowhere else for him to go. Already the spongy head of his penis pushed against her cervix. The sweet torturous pressure of him there had her wanting to grind her body to his.

He pushed her up and then let her sink back down on him over and over until Granger stilled them, pressing against her back until she lay flush against Marty's chest. The other man wrapped his arms around her, holding her tightly. She wasn't sure if he just enjoyed the feel of her breasts pressed to his chest, or if he were simply holding her still while Granger prepared her for his cock.

Anticipation of what was to come had her shaking. Marty rubbed up and down her back, whispering soothing words in her ear. All the while, Granger massaged the globes of her ass, spreading light kisses across them.

"Your ass is so pretty, Destiny. I love squeezing these cheeks and seeing my handprint change from white to red for a brief second." His voice was so soft she barely heard it.

Then he rubbed something greasy around her back hole, circling it over and over again. It wasn't long before he was pressing inward on the tiny rosette, adding a slight pressure as he slowly entered her with the tip of one finger. Then more of the oil he was using dribbled down the crack of her ass to be pressed inside.

"That's the hottest thing I've ever seen, baby. Your ass taking my finger so perfectly," he said.

She moaned as he moved the finger in and out of her back hole several times. Then he added more lube, and a second finger joined the first. The pressure increased until both fingers popped through the tight, resistant ring. She panted through it as he stretched her with his fingers until she was moaning at the pressure.

"She's ready, Marty." The strain in Granger's voice told her how turned on he was.

Granger removed his fingers, leaving her feeling empty despite Marty's dick piercing her cunt. Before she could say anything, Granger's thick cock was pressing against her dark hole, the insistent press of the thick shaft tearing a gasp from her. It was so much more than his fingers had been. How would he ever fit? She wanted to tell him to stop, that she couldn't handle that much pain, but then he was inside of her, the ring relaxing and letting him in.

"Fuck! So good. So damn hot and tight," Granger whispered in a tight voice.

He filled her all the way to his balls, his chest pressed against her back now. She was so full. Destiny couldn't imagine feeling anything but them ever again. They filled her to overflowing, and it felt perfect. The intimacy was even more than she'd both hoped for and feared. His breath at her neck, the bare skin of his chest with its dusting of hair against her back had her imagining him inside of her head, privy to her ever thought. Fear laced through her that he would know everything about her, setting her heart into a pounding rhythm while her lungs seized. Then he started moving, pulling out as Marty surged up and inside of her. The feeling passed, and she could breathe again.

"Aw, hell. So good, so fucking good, baby." Granger's strained voice echoed her own thoughts at the sensation of one cock pushing inside of her as another one pulled back, awakening nerve endings she hadn't felt before.

"Fuck, Granger. I can feel you moving inside of her. She's so damn tight." Marty's voice sounded just as tense as the other man's did.

"Are you okay, baby?" Granger asked, between wet kisses down her spine.

"Yesss," she hissed out. She couldn't form a complete sentence with the intensity of emotions and physical sensations running like wildfire through her body.

He chuckled, the sound and movement traveling down his body to add a new dimension to the feel of his cock. She groaned and tried to concentrate on breathing. Between Marty's dick in her pussy and Granger's thick cock buried in her ass, it was as if her instincts that kept her heart beating and her lungs seeking oxygen no longer worked right.

The two men moved in tandem, seesawing in and out of her body, spreading friction thick like molasses through her bloodstream. She could taste the pleasure on her tongue, a tease of what was to come. She could feel it building inside of her like a slowly growing ball of sensation that she knew would be beyond anything she'd ever felt before. The leading edge of it felt like a hot wind promising a soothing rain storm in its wake.

Marty held her slightly away from him as he licked and sucked on her nipples. His teeth lightly grazing the hard nubs gave her more stimulation to process among the rest. It wouldn't take much for her to become overloaded with it all. She wasn't sure how much more she could take before she exploded from the sheer pleasure that was growing fast inside of her.

"Ah, hell, Granger. I'm not going to last. She's squeezing me like a vise." Marty's groaned out admission had her clamping down on both men out of reaction.

"Hell, Destiny. Stop that, baby." Granger slipped one hand between her and Marty, his fingers finding her clit with unerring accuracy.

She cried out when he began a soft rub across the sensitive nub.

"That's it, baby. Come for us. Give us what we want, darling."

He tapped the little bundle of nerves, and she exploded around them, her body flying apart in a million different directions. As she convulsed around them, her body milking them as she did, they shouted out their own releases, filling her with their hot cum.

She shuddered as her body slowly came down from the pleasure-induced high they'd created. Every muscle ached from the explosive release. She didn't think she could lift her head, much less move if they asked her to. If someone attacked them right then, she would be helpless to fight them off.

The men didn't seem to be in much better shape, because it was a long time before they slipped from inside of her and settled her between them to sleep. She prayed that they were safe until the next morning. It was the best she could do in her present condition.

Chapter Seventeen

Marty and Granger had argued earlier about what direction to take. The other man wanted to continue west, while he wanted to locate one of the communities closer by and get settled somewhere. He was worried about the weather growing colder and getting caught unprepared by a snowstorm. The weather was unpredictable out here under the best of circumstances.

Granger had finally worn him down, and they were going to drive another day before they searched for a place to settle down. His friend was convinced that they would be safer farther west. While he had his doubts they would be safe anywhere, he let the other man talk him into it since Granger had been out this way and he hadn't.

He glanced up to the mirror to see how Destiny was doing. She'd abandoned her book and was asleep, or resting her eyes. She looked better than she had when they'd first found her, but she was still too thin and there were still circles beneath her eyes. She was amazing, though. Despite having been raised a virtual prisoner by circumstances in her aunt and uncle's home and never allowed to go outside for fear of being taken, she was a wealth of information. She'd have nothing but time to read and study the books they'd gotten for her.

"What are you thinking about?" Granger asked in a soft voice.

"She's special, Granger."

"Yeah." The other man turned and studied her for a few seconds. "That's why I want to look farther north for a place to live. She deserves the chance to live a little without being constantly hidden away inside to keep her safe. I don't know how long it will last, but for a while, anyway, she'll have that freedom to move around some out here."

"I just hope we find a place soon. The air is a lot cooler during the day than it's been." Marty looked up at the clouds building in the distance.

"We're getting close to Yellowstone now, Marty. We'll find somewhere soon. I've been looking at the maps, and there's a lot of cabins and such along the Yellowstone River. I think that's our best bet to find a place to settle down. There should be people in that area."

"I hope you're right. I wish we'd started this trip in the spring instead of the fall," Marty muttered.

"Guess we didn't have much of a choice, Marty. Wishing for something we don't have any control over isn't helping things." Granger glared at him.

Marty sighed. "You're right. Sorry. I'm just on edge. I've been through the winter back there"—he nodded his head behind him— "and it was hard enough then. I can't imagine what it's going to be like out here. Plus, we're farther north than we were to begin with."

"I know, but we're safer out here. If it was just me, I'd move deeper north, but it would be too hard on Destiny." Granger stared back at the still-sleeping woman.

"Um, she's been moving sort of stiff the last few days. Do you think we hurt her the other night?" Marty asked.

It had been bothering him ever since they'd taken her together that maybe it wasn't the right thing to do. He worried that Granger was too much for Destiny, that his need to take her that way was based on what had happened to him in prison somehow. He hadn't broached the subject with the other man because they hadn't really had the opportunity to talk alone before now.

Granger stared at him for a long, silent minute. "Are you really saying that maybe *I* hurt her the other night, Marty?"

"That's not what I asked. Don't go putting words in my mouth, man." Guilt ate at Marty's insides. Guilt over using Destiny like they had, and guilt over thinking that Granger might hurt her even accidently.

"It's what you meant, Marty. I can see it in your eyes." Granger's voice had tightened, sounding cold.

"I'm just saying that maybe *we* were too hard on her. Anal sex isn't exactly something that most women enjoy, and she was a freaking virgin when we met her all of, what, a week ago. Maybe you're moving too fast, Granger." Marty felt marginally better for having gotten it out, but he hated putting his fears into words at the same time.

"And how would you know what most women enjoy when it comes to anal sex, Marty? I got the impression it wasn't something you've ever tried before."

Marty glared over at the other man. He'd almost implied that Marty didn't know much about women or sex. It burned his ass that the other man could read him so well. No, he probably didn't have as much sexual experience as Granger had, but that didn't mean he didn't listen to what others said.

"No, I've never done that before, but I listened to others talk. And my sister and I were once pretty close. I'm not ignorant about the subject of sex, or even anal sex. I just don't see why, if it's not something most women enjoy, you are so serious about it. If Destiny doesn't really like it, are you going to be able to give it up, or is it something you can't live without?"

"What the hell? Marty, if she didn't like it, she wouldn't have had the best damn orgasm she'd ever had before. What is this really about?"

Marty struggled to put into words what was bothering him. He liked Granger. The man knew how to handle himself, and beneath all of the gruffness, he had a heart of gold. But there was a wildness about him that worried Marty. He didn't want Destiny hurt.

"I think you're too hard on her sometimes, is all. She's not a woman who's been around men before. She was a virgin when we found her, Granger. You all but run over her sometimes. Maybe we shouldn't have pushed her into taking both of us together like that until we'd settled down and had a real home around her, maybe other women for her to talk to."

The muscles around Granger's jaw worked as he seemed to struggle to remain in control. Marty watched the man in his peripheral vision as his friend worked at reigning in his emotions. It had obviously struck a nerve with Granger that he hadn't lashed out at him immediately. Marty expected the other man to throw a punch despite the fact that Granger was driving.

"I would never harm her, Marty. She's my life. If you don't like the idea of sharing her with me, you need to come right out and say it, because I'm not giving her up for you or anyone."

Marty's head jerked toward Granger, surprise clogging his throat. He hadn't expected the other man to think he didn't want to share her with him. Yeah, in a perfect world he would have wanted her all to himself, but he loved her too much to risk her life because he was too possessive to want her safe.

"I don't expect you to, Granger. She needs you as much as she needs me. That's not what I was saying at all." Marty ran a hand through his hair and sighed. "I've always associated anal sex with degradation. It was something men enjoyed to prove their dominance over someone, man or woman. It isn't normally very enjoyable for a woman, and asking someone to endure it just because I liked it seems selfish to me. I wouldn't force a woman to swallow if she didn't want to either."

"So you think I like anal sex because it makes me feel superior or something?" Granger's expression hadn't changed. He still appeared cold and indifferent to Marty's insinuations.

"I don't know what you think, Granger. I just know how it looks, what it suggests."

Granger looked back at their woman, sleeping quietly. Marty could see a soft smile on her face as if her dreams were pleasant for a change. He glanced at Granger and saw the softness for her there before he masked it once again and turned back around.

"Just because I was raped in prison doesn't mean I'm too damaged to know what I really feel, Marty. I enjoy anal sex because it feels amazing. I liked it before I ever went to prison. I like the intimacy of it, how it shows the ultimate in trust when a woman allows you to take her that way. I like the way it bonds the three of us when we are all three joined like that. We feel more like a family in that moment than in any other." He stared out the passenger window.

Marty felt like a total asshole at the depth of emotion that finally slipped free of Granger's ironclad hold. It was obvious the other man felt deeply about them as a unit.

"To answer your question, Marty, if Destiny didn't like anal sex, I could do without it and would. She's more important to me than sex, period. But sex is a part of any relationship, even the lack of it. It's part of what binds people together or tears them apart. If she didn't like anal sex, I would never bring it up again."

The silence in the Jeep grew thick and palpable to him as he drove. Granger didn't say another word the rest of the day until they reached an intersection and he told Marty to turn right. Thirty minutes later, Granger pulled the map back out and stared at it. After a few minutes, he looked back up and sighed.

"There are three roads coming up in the next few minutes. All three roads lead to different areas with houses and such on them. I'm not sure which one to pick. I think the best one is the last one because it will be closer to the river and afford a better chance of fresh water and fishing," Granger told him.

"Then what's the problem? Why aren't you settled on that one then?"

"I'm not sure of the type houses there. It may be a primitive area with the bare minimum of living conditions. That's not what we need so close to winter."

"So, we go there and check them out. If they aren't what we want, we spend the night and backtrack to the next set tomorrow," Marty said.

"That's what I had about settled on, but those clouds worry me. They look too much like snow clouds to me. You've had the heater on all day, haven't you? That last time we stopped to syphon gas it was nippy out, and I was wearing a coat." Granger stared at the map once again.

"I vote for the road closest to the river. We'll make the best of whatever we end up with," Marty told him with a sigh.

"Okay. Then turn left at the third road you come to. It looks to be a gravel road according to the map. I hope it's gravel and not dirt, or it won't bode well for the type of accommodations waiting at the end of the line."

When Marty reached the third turn off, he sighed at the sight of gravel and turned down the road. Almost immediately, Destiny woke up with the change to the uneven road.

"Hey, where are we?" she asked in a husky voice.

"Almost home, ladybug." Marty smiled at her in the mirror.

Almost immediately her eyes brightened and sleep fell away. He liked seeing her smile, loved hearing her laugh. He glanced over at Granger and found the other man staring out the side window. He'd created a rift between them that he had to figure out how to fix. They couldn't afford to have it stretching between them.

Thirty minutes later it started to rain. Great big fat drops that seemed to have more weight to them than he would expect splattered the windshield as the trees around them swayed in the rising wind. He was having trouble negotiating the road in the downpour, and the wind only added to the problem. His fingers cramped from gripping the wheel so tightly, but it took holding it that way to keep from ending up in a ditch or careening into a tree. He prayed one of those massive things didn't fall either on them or in front of them.

A few times, they seemed to be driving parallel to the river, worrying him that he'd lose control and they'd end up in the water. If that happened, they didn't stand a chance in hell of survival. The one good thing about the state of the world was that he was pretty certain they wouldn't be meeting any other cars on the road, which meant he was fairly safe driving down the center.

"How much longer 'til we get there?" Destiny called over the noise of the wind and rain.

"Hard to tell," Granger said. "With the weather like this, I can't tell how far we've driven. I think we're nearly there."

Almost like he'd called it up, they emerged into a clearing with a large building looming ahead of them. He could see a flickering light in one of the windows. Slowing down, Marty looked over toward Granger.

"Looks like someone lives there. Do we stop, or do we keep driving and look for another place?"

A tree fell off to the side, barely missing them. Destiny screamed when some of the limbs brushed the side of the Jeep.

"We can't keep driving in this," Granger said. "Let's go see if they are friend or foe."

* * * *

Destiny gripped the seatbelt with both hands as they pulled up in front of the large building. It looked a lot like some of the ski lodges she'd seen in books she'd read. It was much too large to be one person's home since they weren't in any of the larger cities like Hollywood, where people had ridiculously large houses. The door swung open, and an enormous man stood staring out at them with a gun that was much larger than Granger's rifle. It looked like a shotgun from what she'd read.

"I'm going to step out and talk to the man. You two sit tight," Granger said.

"He's got a really big gun, Granger. What if he shoots you?" Destiny didn't want him taking the chance. "Let's just leave and find another place."

"It's okay, darling. I'll be fine. You just sit tight. Marty, if anything happens..."

"I know. Be careful, man."

The look Granger gave him seemed odd to her. What was going on? She didn't like this one bit. Granger opened the door and held his hands up as he got out into the blinding rain. She started shaking, worrying that any second she'd hear the sound of a gun going off.

With the wind and rain as loud as it was, she couldn't hear anything and could barely see Granger as he slowly walked toward the strange man. Then he disappeared altogether when he stepped inside.

"Marty?"

"Shhh, honey. He'll be fine. They're just talking. If they'd been going to shoot him, they wouldn't have allowed him inside the place." Marty's voice sounded confident, but she wasn't feeling the same.

After what felt like forever to her, the door opened and Granger ran back out to the Jeep. Marty unlocked the door just as the other man reached it and snatched it open. Granger climbed inside, an umbrella in his hand.

"They're going to let us stay with them temporarily while we finish fixing a cabin close by they've been working on. The men aren't real comfortable with us, so go slow. They have a child and their woman, so they're cautious," Granger told them. "Marty, we'll grab the packs. Destiny, take the umbrella so you don't get too wet. With the wind like it is, I'm not sure it's going to help much."

Destiny was excited to be staying somewhere other than abandoned buildings for a change, but she was nervous about meeting the others. Granger had said to be careful, so that meant he wasn't one hundred percent sure of their welcome. When he opened her door, she was ready, opening the umbrella and jumping out at the same time. She ran for the door and was instantly plucked from the rain by a mountain of a man. He set her down and took the umbrella from her.

She looked way up at him and quickly took a step back. The man had to be six and a half feet or more. His shaggy black hair and equally dark eyes frightened her. When he turned away from her to close the door once Marty and Granger were inside once again, she breathed a sigh of relief. Marty and Granger quickly pulled her behind them.

"Thank you for letting us stay tonight," Marty said.

The big man grunted but didn't say anything more. They stood staring at each other in silence until the sound of someone hurrying down the stairs had him turning in a flash.

"Abe, stop glaring at them. They're soaked to the skin and need to dry off." The sound of a woman's voice had Destiny peering around Marty's side.

The woman standing in front of the giant looked tiny compared to the big man. Her light brown eyes sparkled with amusement as she looked up at him. Poking him in the chest, she walked around him, but he pulled her back into his arms.

"Hi, I'm Celina and this is Abe, one of my husbands. Russell is upstairs getting your room ready." Her sweet smile made Destiny feel slightly less fearful of the giant of a man behind her.

"I'm Granger, and this is Marty, and our woman, Destiny," Granger told them.

Destiny noticed that Celina was about three inches taller than she was. The woman's smile was infectious, and she found herself smiling back. She started to slip around Marty's side to say hello, but he kept her behind him. When she would have said something to him about letting her go, another man descended the stairs carrying a child who looked no more than five or six months old. She had a head full of honey-blonde hair that looked soft as a cloud.

"Your room is ready. The bathroom is open to the room on the other side, but you can lock the door if you feel more comfortable. There's no one here but us, though." The man shifted the child in his arms.

"This is Russell. The young woman behind them is their woman, Destiny," Celina told him.

Russell nodded toward them, then handed the baby to Abe. "I'll show you the way."

They followed him toward the stairs, the light from the roaring fire in the fireplace lighting their way. Destiny looked back to see Abe talking softly to Celina with a stern expression on his face. The woman laughed and hugged him. Evidently she wasn't scared of him.

When they reached the landing, Russell grabbed a lantern sitting on a table and led them down the hall to one of the rooms with the door open.

"Here you go, keep the lantern. I'll grab another one. When you're dry and ready to come downstairs, we'll fix something to eat and talk." With that, Russell left them in the hall and disappeared into the darkness.

Granger hurried her into the room behind Marty and closed the door behind them. Marty set the lantern on the dresser in front of the mirror, and the two men began rummaging through the packs for dry clothes.

"Get out of those clothes, ladybug. I'll grab a towel and dry you off." Marty hurried into the bathroom and returned with several towels.

They all stripped and quickly dried off, then dressed in dry clothes. She hung their wet things around the room to dry while Granger draped the towels in the bathroom to dry. The sight of the bed looking all comfortable and inviting sent a longing inside of her she hadn't realized she had. It had been several nights since they'd slept on a real bed. She was eager to climb into this one.

"Let's go on downstairs. I want Destiny in front of that fire so she doesn't catch cold," Granger said.

Marty grabbed the lantern, and they filed out of the room and down the hall to the stairs. Granger immediately put her next to the railing and made sure she gripped it as they descended the steps. She wasn't sure whether to feel annoyed or cherished. Before she could dwell on it too long, Granger was pulling her in front of the fireplace.

Abe and Russell sat in chairs on either side of a comfortable looking couch. The child lay in Abe's arms, playing with the button on his shirt. The sight of the big man holding the child so carefully melted some of her initial fear of him. He couldn't be all bad if he took care of the child, could he? His eyes twinkled when they looked down at the baby in his arms. They changed when he glanced over at them.

Granger stood a little in front of her while Marty rubbed up and down her arms. She couldn't help but enjoy the feel of the heat from the fire against her skin. She'd been colder than she realized. Getting wet hadn't been a good thing.

"Dinner is almost ready, everyone. Come on into the kitchen." Celina's voice carried across the room to them.

Russell had jumped up and hurried toward the kitchen as if putting himself between them and his wife in case they meant any harm. Destiny hated that they had to be so suspicious of them, but she could understand. Trusting people you didn't know was dangerous in this day and age. It would take time for them to accept them. That is, if they were allowed to stay in the general area.

Once they entered the kitchen, the mood began to lighten. Abe settled the child into what appeared to be a handmade highchair. He sat on one side of her, and Celina took the other chair. Russell sat on the other side of Celina.

The woman looked up and smiled at them. "Have a seat."

Granger had her sit at the other end of the table with him and Marty sitting on either side of her. This put her and Celina at the two ends. They smiled at each other. It wasn't lost to either of them what the men were doing.

"Your daughter is beautiful. What is her name?" Destiny asked.

"Bethany Ann. We call her Beth," Celina told them.

"Sweet Pea, more often than not," Russell added with a snort.

Celina sighed and rolled her eyes. "She's going to think her name is Sweet Pea if you aren't careful. Then what will you do?"

"How old is she?" Destiny asked, watching as the baby slapped her hands on the tray part of the chair.

"She's five months old, and such a sweet baby." Celina rubbed her fingers over the child's arm. Turning back to them, she grinned. "Don't just sit there, dig in."

For the next few minutes, they passed around the food. Destiny's mouth watered at the sight of what looked like some sort of roast and potatoes. It had been a long time since she'd had anything other than jerky or beans for protein. Her stomach growled appreciatively, embarrassing her to no end. Everyone laughed, and they started talking while they ate, the tension easing a bit.

"Where are you from?" Russell asked.

"I'm originally from Chicago, Destiny is from Atlanta, and Granger is from Boston," Marty told them.

"We decided it was safer to move as far west as possible. The black market agents are a law unto themselves and don't care who they kill to get what they want," Granger told them.

"We haven't had problems with them this far west yet, but that won't last," Abe said in a gruff voice. "Our biggest dangers out here are wild animals and the elements. You've got to be able to work to make it out here."

"We expected that. I've lived almost this far before. I know the challenges. We'll make it," Granger told the man.

"You picked a bad time to make the trip. You should have waited until spring. How do you expect to live through the winter?" Abe asked.

"We've got enough supplies if we're careful, and we can supplement it with fresh game." Granger met the other man's eyes without flinching.

Destiny hated the tension growing once again. She understood that they were in a precarious situation, but she hated that her men were being challenged like this.

"They didn't have a choice of when to travel. They were trying to keep me safe," she blurted out.

"Destiny," Granger began.

"If it wasn't for me, you wouldn't be in this situation." She felt tears pricking the back of her eyelids.

Marty reached over and pulled her hand into his. "Hush, honey. It's not your fault. We did what we had to do."

"Are you in some kind of trouble?" Abe demanded, dropping his fork to the plate. "Did you lead danger to my family's door?"

Chapter Eighteen

"No. No one is after us," Granger said with a sigh. "When we met Destiny, she was traveling as a teenage boy, trying to stay hidden. She had no family and was a sitting duck like she was."

"That's why your hair is cut so short," Celina said. "I had wondered why you would cut such beautiful hair like that."

"I didn't know what else to do." She hated remembering those first few weeks, when she was so scared she couldn't eat, even when she did have food.

"How did you three meet?" Russell asked.

Granger quickly recounted the story, hitting the highlights and leaving out much of the more personal parts. When he finished, everyone was quiet.

"I can't even begin to imagine what life was like for you, Destiny. Going from living almost like a prisoner without even being allowed outside for fresh air to being thrust into the world we live in now and forced to pretend to be a boy to survive. It's a miracle you survived, and a blessing you found these two men to care for you." Celina's eyes were bright with tears for her.

Destiny couldn't miss the compassion in the other woman's eyes. She hoped they would be staying there and become friends. Celina was several years older than her mere twenty-two, but she felt as if they already shared a bond.

"We have several good-sized cabins that we've been working on as we had time. They can all easily be added on to if the need arises, but it will take time to get one ready. I honestly don't think we'll have time to finish one before the snow starts," Russell said.

"They can stay with us this winter," Abe said in a gruff voice. "We've got plenty of room, and the women will probably enjoy having each other's company."

"We appreciate your willingness to open your home to us, Abe. Marty and I will work on the cabin while the weather allows and help around the lodge wherever you need help," Granger told him.

Destiny had noticed that he'd been acting differently toward her ever since she'd woken up. He seemed almost distant and careful around her. She couldn't help but wonder why. Just when she thought everything was going so well, something changed between them. She would find out what was wrong and fix it. Her men were too important in her life to lose them for any reason.

After they'd eaten, she helped Celina clean up. Her men took little Beth with them into the living room as the men all filed out of the room. Destiny listened as Celina talked about living out there and the hard work ahead of them with winter on the way.

"You have to keep the cattle fed and close together, as well as the horses and our few chickens." She dried her hands on a towel then started setting up the coffee pot.

Destiny was thrilled that they had gas for the stove, though Celina said they didn't expect it to last much longer. She'd said that there wasn't anyone this far west to keep them supplied with it like there was back east. The other woman motioned for her to sit at the table.

"I wanted to talk to you about your men. They treat you well, don't they?" she asked with a serious expression on her face.

"Yes! They're great to me. Why?" Destiny wasn't sure why the other woman was asking her.

"Well, sometimes men will just use a woman for their needs and not treat her well. I know you said you'd been living like a boy before you met them, but you're so thin and have bruises on you. I wanted to be sure they aren't abusing you, is all."

Destiny fought down the urge to tell her to mind her own business. It was sweet that Celina cared, and she was only trying to make sure she wasn't being abused. Not many people would care, much less speak up and ask these days. She calmed herself and smiled at her.

"I'm fine. I'm much better than I was when they found me. I'd been badly beaten and starved, with barely enough to survive. They've treated me with nothing but kindness and are constantly urging me to eat. I'm slowly eating more as I can. I'd been eating so little for so long that I've had to work myself back up to it."

"I'm glad to hear they are good to you. If anything ever changes, you know you can come to me, and my men will make sure you're safe. They would never allow a woman to be abused, Destiny." She stood up and checked on the coffee water. "Looks like it's about ready. Let's carry it in the other room and join the men."

* * * *

"It's getting late. We'd better all get some rest," Abe said, standing up and stretching.

Celina had already taken the baby upstairs and put her to bed. They'd all been sitting around talking about everything, from the past to what life was like this far west. Abe and Russell seemed to have accepted them and didn't appear as reserved as before. Destiny could only pray that everything worked out. She couldn't shake the feeling that something was going on between Granger and Marty. They'd seemed to be avoiding each other despite sitting on either side of her.

"You're right. We need to check out the cabin tomorrow and see what needs to be done." Granger held out his hand to Abe. "We appreciate you all giving us a chance to live here. I know it's not easy to trust strangers."

Abe shook his hand and then Marty's. He nodded at them before wrapping an arm around Celina and leading the way upstairs. Russell doubled back, saying he was going to check all the doors again before coming up. It gave Destiny a little more confidence that this was the right place for them.

The heat of Marty's hand at her back as they climbed the stairs together was comforting when everything else inside of her screamed that something was wrong. Granger had taken the lead for them and carried the lantern as they walked across the landing to their room. When he opened the door and disappeared inside, Destiny followed the dancing light into the room and watched as Granger set it on the dresser in front of the mirror and started undressing. When neither man said anything after Marty closed the door, Destiny knew she'd been right. Something was definitely going on between them.

"Granger? What's going on?" she asked, walking over to touch his arm.

He looked at her with a blank expression. "Nothing, darling. What do you mean?"

She searched his eyes, but nothing shown in their obsidian darkness. Turning, she walked to where Marty was pulling off his shirt on the other side of the bed. He actually flinched when she stayed his hand from unfastening his jeans.

"Marty?"

"What, honey?"

"Are you and Granger fighting about something? Did I do something to upset y'all?" she asked.

He immediately pulled her into his arms. "No, ladybug. You haven't done anything wrong. Why would you think that?"

"Because something is eating you two. You're dancing around each other like you're afraid you're going to get cooties or something. What is it? What has you both acting like this?" She turned to Granger. "You've barely touched me all night. What else am I supposed to think?" Destiny pulled away from him and turned to stare at both men.

Neither man moved. Neither man said a word. They just stared at each other and then her. Destiny huffed out a breath and crossed her arms. They weren't going to bed until they'd at least told her what was going on. The longer they let things fester inside, the worse it would get, and the harder it would be to fix things in the long run.

"I'm not budging until someone tells me what in the hell is going on." When they still remained stubbornly quiet, she growled and threw up her hands in defeat. "If you want to go to bed, then climb in, but you're going to be sleeping with each other because I'm going back downstairs to sleep on the couch."

With that, she turned around and marched to the door. When she grasped the doorknob, prepared to fling the door open, strong arms grabbed her from behind and lifted her off her feet.

Granger.

"Put me down, Granger! I'm not sleeping in here with two stubborn, ornery assholes who are too manly to speak up." She struggled, but he only threw her on the bed.

"This is what's wrong, Destiny. I'm a rough man. I like sex, and I like it nasty. You don't deserve to be treated that way, and I get that, but it doesn't change what I like and want." Granger panted when he'd finished.

"So? Have I complained about anything? You haven't hurt me or disgusted me. Are you feeling guilty about what we did the other night? 'Cause if you are, you shouldn't be. There's nothing to feel bad about. I loved every minute of it." She looked from him to Marty, and it suddenly hit her. Her mouth opened and then closed again with the knowledge of what the issue was. She eased off the bed and stared at the other man.

"Marty? Granger doesn't feel guilty, but you do, don't you." She made it a statement, knowing the answer already.

"Honey, I..."

She stopped him. "I want to know how you feel about what we did. Did you enjoy it or hate it?" she asked. Destiny couldn't control the tremble in her voice or the tears fighting to fall.

"That's just it," Marty finally said in a soft voice. "I liked it. Too much. It's not right, Destiny. It's degrading for Granger to take you that way."

"Funny. I don't feel degraded. I'd think that since it happened to me, that I would be the one to feel that way, don't you? Granger wasn't treating me like a worthless bitch, or even a whore. He cares about me. I never once felt like I was being used." She shook her head and looked down at her feet. "At least I didn't until you suggested that I was."

"No! You're not any of those things. Hell, I don't know what to do. But watching Granger take you like he did bothers me," Marty said.

"Because you fucking liked it," Granger said with a growl in his voice. "And that makes you more like me than you want to be. I'm an ex-con, rough around the edges, and abrasive. You think better of yourself than that, and it pisses you off that maybe you're just as perverted as you think I am. Well, fuck you, Marty." Granger's voice had grown deeper but louder.

"Hold it down, Granger," Destiny cautioned the big man. She turned to Marty, unsure what to say now. "I love you, Marty. I love Granger, too. Just because he likes kinky sex, it doesn't make him a bad person. I know he'd never do anything to hurt me. I trust him, just like I trust you. It sounds like you're angrier with yourself than you are with Granger. Taking it out on him isn't fair, Marty."

"Hell, I know that." He ran a hand through his wavy hair and pulled at it. "It just feels wrong to enjoy—that," he finally said.

Granger sneered. "Anal sex? Rough sex? Just what is *that*?"

"Granger. You're not helping things," Destiny cautioned.

"No, he's right, honey. I was raised to never harm a woman and that some things were just wrong on principal, like," he swallowed, "anal sex and stuff like that."

"Like spanking your sweet ass, darling, or tying your up so you have to take all the pleasure we give you," Granger told her. "He thinks that anything except plain old missionary sex is dirty and wrong."

"No, I don't. It's just that some of the things you like seem a little extreme." He cursed and leaned back against the wall, closing his eyes. "I almost hate myself for wanting those things with you, Destiny. I love you, and the thought of ever hurting you makes me physically ill just thinking about it."

She walked over to stand in front of Marty. Lifting her hands, she cupped his face in them and stared into his eyes.

"But Marty, you're not hurting me, or using me, or any of those things you're scared of when it's what I want. If I didn't like or want something you guys did to me, believe me, you wouldn't do it again." She smiled up at him. "I love you both. I want both of you to make love to me at the same time sometimes. I want to feel you both deep inside of me, binding us together as a family. I like having my ass spanked sometimes. Nothing either of you has ever done to me or *threatened* me with scares me or turns me off. I'd tell you, Marty."

He stared down at her and covered her hands on his face with his own. She could see the struggle in his eyes, but finally he closed them and nodded. Relief flooded her chest. She knew it wasn't the end of it, but it was a step in the right direction.

Destiny dropped her hands and turned to walk over to where Granger stood with both hands fisted at his waist, wearing only his boxer briefs hung low on his narrow hips. She searched his eyes, hating the wary way he watched her approach him. Stopping in front of him, close enough she could take a deep breath and her breasts would brush against his chest, Destiny closed her eyes and inhaled his scent, the rich, spicy aroma that was unique to Granger. Opening her eyes once again, she smiled up at him.

"I'd tell you, too, Granger. I don't want you to be anyone except who you are, inside and out." She placed her hands against his chest, soaking in the warmth and comfort that just touching him gave her. "I don't want anything between us, guys. This has to stop. We talk about everything together, or it will never work."

Granger uncurled his fists and rested them lightly at her waist. "I love you, baby. You deserve better than this, but it's who I am and fuck it, I can't let you go."

Another set of hands rested on her shoulders, and the press of Marty's hard body against her back, his hard cock nestled against her lower back, let her know he wanted everything to be good between them. Destiny leaned her head back against his chest and lightly scored her nails down Granger's rock hard chest.

"Strip, Destiny," Granger said, his voice deep and raspy.

When his eyes dropped to half-mast, she knew he was right there with her.

Chapter Nineteen

Destiny shivered at the sound of Granger's rough voice. She slowly unbuttoned her shirt, taking her time as she did. Marty walked around her to stand next to Granger so he had a clear view of her as she slowly revealed the plain white bra she wore. After she dropped her blouse to the floor, she slid her hands down her chest, over her bra, and down her belly to rest at the waistband of her jeans.

"Take them off, darling. All of them." Granger didn't move as he watched her slowly unfasten her jeans, sliding the zipper down.

When she started to slide them down her hips, Marty stopped her.

"Turn around and take them off real slow," he said.

She bit back a smile and slowly turned around. She quickly kicked off her shoes then slipped her hands inside the waistband and shoved them down one slow inch at a time. When she got them just past her hips, she bent over and pushed them down to her ankles, making sure they got a good view of her panty-covered ass for a few seconds before she stood back up and stepped out of the pants.

She had to roll in her lips and bite them to keep from laughing at the sound of one of them hissing out a breath when she reached around and unfastened the clasps of her bra. She slipped her arm out of one strap at a time before pulling it off and holding the plain white garment out to one side and letting it drop to the floor. Then she once again slipped her hands down her sides and into the waistband of her panties and rolled them down her legs as she bent over until she was able to step out of first one side and then the other. Instead of standing back up, she slowly spread her legs and grasped her ankles, letting them see her—all of her.

"Fuck me," Marty gasped.

She slid a finger between her legs and dragged it all around her pussy without touching the wet folds or her sensitive clit. The more she stroked around her wet hole, the more she heard the men's heavy breathing behind her. When she slipped her finger over her entrance and let it hover there, Granger growled low in his throat.

"Do it."

She moaned and slowly sank her finger deep into her pussy over and over, then rolled it over her clit. She couldn't stop her hips from swaying as she pumped her finger in and out of her hot, wet cunt.

"Aw, hell, baby," Granger said, just before he grabbed her hips and pulled her back against him. "Marty, pull back the covers."

He pulled her up, holding her until she was steady, then turned her around and took her mouth in an almost-punishing kiss. He owned her mouth as he touched and tortured every single inch of it. His tongue licked and stroked hers, sending shivers down her spine. What was it about their kisses that always made her dizzy?

When he finally pulled away, both of them were panting and shaking. He skimmed over her shoulders and down her arms until he reached her hands, where he laced their fingers together. As he drew her over to the edge of the bed, she caught a glimpse of Marty, gloriously naked, wearing only a smile as he knelt on the opposite side.

"Climb over to the center of the bed and lay on your back, arms over your head, and grasp the mattress. Don't let go of it for any reason, baby." Granger smiled down at her, but it held a wealth of heat that had her tingling in all the right places.

With one more look into his bottomless eyes, Destiny climbed onto the bed and eased to the middle, where she lay back and lifted her arms over her head. She grasped the edges of the mattress with her hands and waited.

"Spread your legs," Marty said.

She moved them apart.

"More," Granger growled.

Destiny spread them wide, no longer wanting to play around. She was aching for their touch, needing to feel their skin next to hers. Waiting was killing her. She turned her head to look at Granger, but suddenly he was there next to her, stretched out by her side without touching her. The bed dipped on the other side and Marty lay next to her. Cocooned in their body heat without the benefit of their body, Destiny wanted to beg them to touch her, but she held her tongue, waiting to see what they would do next.

As if they'd discussed it earlier, both men rolled closer and closed their mouths over a taut nipple. The feel of their mouths drawing on the tight peaks without the benefit of their touch anywhere else left her a little disoriented and unsure. They grasped her nipples with their teeth then teased them with their tongues. The confusing sensations of pain and pleasure had her pussy weeping and her cunt quivering with the need to be filled.

She could no longer hold it in. Her moans filled the room as they sucked on her nipples as if they couldn't get enough. She wanted to dig her hands through their hair, but Granger had said to keep her hands on the mattress. It wasn't fair. She needed to touch them. She needed them to touch her. A soft whimper escaped her mouth.

Granger let go of her throbbing nipple and looked up at her. "What is it, darling?"

"Please. I want to touch you. I need you both. Please let me touch you." Had she not been so turned on and desperate, she would have never begged him like this.

"Don't move those hands, Destiny. We'll take care of you. Patience."

She had none. She wanted it now, not ten or even five minutes from now. Her groan of frustration had both men chuckling around her nipples. Her grip on the mattress grew tighter as she fought against cursing or knocking both of them off the bed.

"Easy, ladybug. Just feel. Soon you'll have everything you wanted." Marty's soothing voice helped settle her some.

Granger released her nipple with a soft pop before leaving soft kisses down her belly to her mound. He slipped between her legs, spreading them wider to accommodate his wide shoulders. She squirmed as his hot breath fanned over her wet folds, stirring her curly pubic hair.

"You smell so damn good, baby. I'm going to eat you up, darling." She nearly screamed when his tongue lapped over her swollen pussy lips.

When he spread her folds with his fingers, Destiny threw her head back in anticipation. With Marty torturing both nipples and Granger teasing her pussy, she didn't stand a chance of lasting very much longer. Her entire body felt like it was on the uphill grind of a rollercoaster about to reach the top and plunge down into the spiraling corkscrew she'd always been afraid of as a young child.

Granger buried his face in her pussy, stabbing her cunt with his tongue and licking up every drop of cream she produced. The pressure of his nose against her clit had her pulsing around him, waiting for that single sensation that would hurtle her over the top in an explosion of pleasure.

He inched her higher as he thrust two fingers inside her, stroking up and rasping over her hot spot at the same time Marty nipped her nipple with his teeth while twisting the other one in his fingers. She screamed and bucked as ecstasy poured through her body like water from a burst dam.

Marty cut off her screams with his mouth after hissing out, "Gonna wake the baby."

Granger chuckled deeply against her pussy then sucked her clit into his mouth, sending another round of tiny climaxes over her. When they both finally released her, Destiny fought to catch her breath. Granger was having none of that. He lifted her legs over the crook of his arms, and, lining his cock up with her slit, he plunged into her quivering cunt like a battering ram. As his dick delved through tender tissues, he reignited the smoldering embers there.

Oh, God. They are going to kill me with pleasure.

Marty knelt by her head and rubbed his cock against her lips. "Open up, honey, and suck my dick."

Destiny opened and ran her tongue all around the crown of his cock before closing her mouth over it. As she stroked his stalk with her tongue, he slowly pumped in and out of her mouth, never going very deep, but keeping a smooth rhythm.

"That's so damn hot, baby. Watching you suck his cock like that. Your lips are stretched wide around him, all swollen and glistening with your saliva." Granger's husky voice thrilled through her system. He sounded so sexy when he was turned on.

"Work her mouth good, Marty, but don't come. I want us both to fill her pussy with our seed. She's ours, Marty. She belongs to us." Granger's declaration filled her with hope and a sense of belonging that she'd lost when she'd lost her freedom.

Marty worked his cock in and out of her mouth. She watched as he squeezed his eyes shut, groaning as she sucked hard on his thick cock, trying to make him come in her mouth. She would give it her best, but she knew he would hold out to be a part of Granger's plan. She wound her tongue all around the shaft as he pumped in and out of her mouth, the skin stretched taut and slick with her saliva.

Granger jerked her attention back to him when he pushed her legs closer to her chest and adjusted his position until now his dick rubbed against her sweet spot every time he tunneled into her cunt. Pressure built inside of her. Everything seemed to narrow down to the feel of Marty thick and hot in her mouth and Granger's relentless pounding in her pussy. She dug her fingers into the mattress, trying to hold on. She felt as if the orgasm building this time would be too big, too overwhelming.

Then Granger was shouting his release, his hot cum filling her womb as his fingers dug into her legs. When he pulled out and knelt, panting, on the bed, Destiny wanted to scream that she hadn't come yet.

Marty pulled from her mouth and laughed. "Granger, if looks could kill, you'd be a dead man right about now. I don't think ladybug appreciates that you left her hanging, man."

"On your hands and knees, babe. It's Marty's turn, and he's going to make sure you come this time." Granger grinned down at her, his eyes appearing sated and sleepy now.

Destiny started to tell him to go fuck himself, but since he'd already come, it wouldn't have had nearly the impact she would have intended for it to.

He popped her on the outside of her thigh. "I said get on your hands and knees. Now, Destiny. That is, if you want to come tonight."

* * * *

Marty bit back a smile when Destiny growled and shot Granger a dirty look before she turned over and got to her hands and knees. Granger popped her on the ass one more time then moved to the side to let Marty slide behind her. The sight of the other man's handprint on her ass should have angered him, but instead, it made him even harder, if that was possible. As he ran his hands over her ass, he felt the heat of the handprint. His cock jerked at the sight of Destiny's pussy, wet and dripping with a combination of hers and Granger's cum.

Marty looked over where Granger was stretched out on his back looking up at Destiny. The man's eyes flicked to him, and a smile crept over his face.

"Take care of our woman, Marty. She needs to come." Granger's words seemed to galvanize him into action.

He took his cock and rubbed it up and down her soaked slit before pushing at it and slowly sinking into her hot depths. The walls of her cunt squeezed him to the point he thought he'd lose it right then.

Marty slowly pulled out and pressed forward again, this time managing to sink all the way inside of her, slapping his balls against her clit.

"Oh, God!" Destiny lowered her head to the mattress.

"Fuck, you're so damn tight, honey. I'm never going to last." Marty tried to keep his strokes slow to keep from blowing too soon, but she felt so good, so right.

He eyed her back hole and how it seemed to wink at him each time he plunged his cock deep inside of her. Marty couldn't stop thinking about it, how tight she'd been when Granger had taken her ass the other day. He didn't want to want that. Didn't want to know what it felt like to be buried in her dark hole, but he couldn't stop thinking about it, either.

He quickly dragged his finger through the cum flowing from her pussy and painted her back hole with it. Then he coated one finger with it and slowly pressed into her tight hole. He remembered how it had felt before when he'd stretched her some. The same secret thrill filled him as he pushed past the slight resistance and filled her with his finger even as his cock filled her pussy.

She hissed out *yes*, letting him know she wanted it. Some of the uneasiness that filled him over his craving her that way eased as it was clear she liked it, liked having her ass filled. He timed his strokes in her ass to the ones he made into her cunt. In then out, slow and easy. She wiggled her behind and groaned.

"Please, Marty. Fuck me. I need to come." Her voice held a hint of impatience.

Marty looked over to find Granger's attention on him. The other man nodded in encouragement. He added a second finger to her ass and immediately felt the difference it made in her pussy around his cock. She groaned again, thrusting her ass back with each pump of his hips and fingers. Over and over, he filled her holes with his dick and fingers. He was so close now. So hard and turned on, riding high on the adrenaline of pleasuring her that he knew he wasn't going to be able to hold out and send her over first without help.

"Granger," he managed to rasp out. "I…"

"I've got her," the other man said and reached beneath Destiny's hips.

Immediately, she clamped down around Marty's cock, a keening cry leaving her lips. He had no doubt Granger was stroking her clit. Marty felt free to pump her pussy and ass in full force now, and he did, pounding into her like a freight train. When she convulsed beneath him, her muffled scream told him she'd reached her peak. It carried him over with her, his balls exploding and sending his cum spewing deep inside of her pussy, filling her womb much as Granger had minutes earlier.

When he pulled out, it took all of his remaining strength not to collapse on top of her. Instead, he hit the other side of the bed and rolled to his side to find that she was still kneeling there with her ass up in the air. He chuckled at the sight. Her mouth held a bite of pillow in it that she'd evidently grabbed to muffle her scream.

He gently removed the pillow and leaned in to kiss her on the cheek. "I love you, Destiny."

She opened eyes that were still slightly glazed with pleasure. She licked her lips and smiled at him. He could see her love for them in her eyes.

"I love you, too, Marty. I love Granger, too, but I don't have the energy to turn my head right now."

Granger's chuckle on the other side made Marty smile even broader. Then he saw the other man's big hand shove at Destiny's ass until it slowly lowered to the bed. The other man sat up and, after smiling down at their woman, reached and pulled the covers from the foot of the bed over all three of them.

"Get some sleep, Marty. I have a feeling we're going to be pretty damn busy tomorrow."

Marty was fairly sure the other man was right. He hoped that everything was going to work out now. He had been an idiot to blame his fear and self-loathing on Granger. It hadn't been fair to the other man. If what they'd done together with Destiny hadn't felt good to her, she would have told them, and they'd have never done it again. He'd known that but had still blundered on like a clumsy bear, accusing Granger of using her to satisfy some sick need inside of him. Well, if it was a sick need, then Marty had the same one inside of him. He owed the other man a sincere apology at the first opportunity he had to talk to him.

"Night, guys," Destiny said in a soft voice.

"Night, ladybug. Sweet dreams," Marty said.

"G'night, baby."

Granger's soft snore seconds later seemed to amuse Destiny. Her quiet laughs eased him into sleep.

Chapter Twenty

"There you go, Destiny. That looks much better. You're getting the hang of it." Celina's praise was comforting to Destiny as she worked on the blanket she was knitting.

"Knitting wasn't one of the things I studied and learned to do when I was growing up. We didn't have real cold winters in Atlanta. I just never thought I'd need to know how to knit." Destiny concentrated on her stitches, afraid she'd drop one when she wasn't supposed to.

"Well, you sure know how to cook. That's for sure. And the fact that you know how to can and put up food is wonderful. Not many people know how to do that anymore. I had to learn when everything went to hell," Celina said.

"Well, my family had always had gardens, and I started learning how to do that when I was a kid anyway. Then after the disasters, my aunt kept me busy in the kitchen all the time. We canned everything you could think of. My uncle smoked meats, and we made jerky and salted bacon and such."

"You've settled in and adjusted really well, Destiny. I'm real proud of you. Not only that, but you've finally gained a little weight. I was so worried that once winter got here you'd end up sick, as thin as you were." Celina's voice was heavy with concern.

"I'm fine. Won't be long until my hair will be as long as Marty's is," she said with a smile.

"I have to say it looks much better since you let me shape it some. Don't ever hack at it like that again!" Celina said with a smile.

Little Beth talked to herself as she played with the toys they'd give her in the playpen the men had made for her. It kept her occupied while keeping her safe. Destiny couldn't get over how comfortable together they'd all grown. It felt wonderful to have friends and another woman to talk to. The men were getting along well and working on their cabin between helping with chores.

She was a little miffed that they hadn't let her see the cabin yet, although they had promised to let her see it before it started snowing. She'd make sure they kept that promise. It didn't matter what it looked like now, she'd be fine and they'd slowly get it like they wanted it. It would just take time.

"Abe says it will snow tomorrow. Are you going to make your guys take you out to see the cabin today?" Celina asked with a smug smile on her face.

"I was just thinking about that. Are you sure it will? It's not really all that cold out there right now."

"Abe always knows when the weather is changing. I'd make sure those men of yours take you tonight, or it might be a while before you can get to go again," Celina said.

"Thanks. I'll make sure they take me over there when they come in for a break. We've been here nearly three weeks now. I'm ready to see what it looks like." Besides, Destiny had something she needed to talk to them about.

"Are you going to tell them?" Celina asked without looking at her.

Destiny frowned. "Tell them what?" she asked.

The other woman smirked. "About the baby."

"Baby? But how did you know?" she nearly yelled.

"I recognized the signs. You've been ill feeling in the mornings and not eating much but make up for it at lunch. I was the opposite. I got sick at night for some odd reason. Then there's the way you've been looking at Beth lately."

"I'm scared, Celina. I don't know anything about having babies. I didn't study much about that." She laid the blanket she'd been working on down and squeezed her hands together. "And what if the guys are upset that I got pregnant so soon?"

"You'll be just fine, Destiny. I'll be here with you. As far as your men are concerned, I expect they'll be excited, but nervous." Celina reached over and squeezed Destiny's hands. "I have a confession to make, though."

Destiny looked over at her. "What?"

"I'm pregnant, too. I haven't told my guys yet either. I was sort of waiting for you to tell yours to tell mine." Celina's soft smile thrilled Destiny.

"You mean we're going to have our babies at the same time?" she squealed.

"Close anyways. I suspect I'm a few weeks ahead of you."

Destiny ran her hand over her own belly and wondered what she would have. Would it be a boy or a girl, and would the guys care? The thought of telling them scared her a little. They had been doing so well lately. Although they did make love to her at the same time, only Granger ever took her in her ass. Marty hadn't wanted to do that yet. She didn't push him, and so neither did Granger. But there seemed to be a closer connection between the three of them now. She loved the way they made her feel and the fact that they were comfortable with each other.

Just as she was about to pick up the knitting again, they heard the men talking just outside the door before it opened to admit the four of them, laughing and talking as they walked inside.

She and Celina got up and walked over to them as they hung up their work coats and stepped out of their boots. Destiny looked up to Abe.

"Did you tell them?" she asked him.

Abe frowned. "Tell who, what?"

"Granger and Marty? Did you tell them it was going to snow tomorrow?" she asked.

Marty looked at Granger. "He mentioned it might snow."

Granger groaned at Destiny's squeal of delight.

"So are you going to take me to see the cabin now?" she demanded.

"Baby, it's not finished. I don't want you to get your hopes up until we get it ready," Granger explained.

Destiny was having none of that. She jumped up into his arms and wrapped hers around his neck. "Please, Granger. I want to see it. I know it's just a hunting cabin and you've had to really do a lot of work on it. I'm not expecting much. I just want to see it. Please?"

Marty chuckled next to them then started laughing hard when Granger turned a sour face toward him.

"Believe me, man. You're going to want to go on and take her to see it now before you find yourself out there in the cold snow later. You will. Take it from us. The women always win," Russell told them.

Destiny watched Granger and Marty exchange glances. She could tell they were going to give in from the way Granger drew in a deep breath and let it out.

"Okay. Let us get some coffee and grab a few things, and we'll go look at it," Granger said with a sigh.

She covered his face in kisses, making everyone laugh. Then she slipped from his arms and grabbed Marty to treat him to the same appreciation. He laughed the entire time.

"Come on, woman. Make us some coffee if you want us to drag your ass back to the cabin," Granger fussed halfheartedly.

Thirty minutes later, the guys bundled her up despite the fact it wasn't all that cold out and led her out the door.

"Remember. Stay right with us and don't wander off. There are wolves and bears out here," Granger warned her.

"I promise, for the fifth time already," she fussed back with a smile.

Marty shook his head at them. He was carrying a backpack and bringing up the rear. They had Destiny between them for safety. She truly doubted there was any need for it, but she wouldn't push her luck by straying. Besides, she had someone else to look out for now. The knowledge that she was carrying a part of one of her men inside of her, growing into a tiny person, not only thrilled her but made her feel different inside as well. She planned to tell them about the baby at the cabin.

When they reached the little bungalow that had been barely visible from the lodge, Granger unlocked the door and walked inside to look around while she remained outside with Marty. They'd just left the place, but Granger insisted on checking it out to be sure.

"Okay. It's fine." He walked back to the door, carrying a lantern even though it was still light out.

She walked inside and smiled at the overly large room that had both the living areas and the kitchen in it. A large fireplace took up a good bit of one wall. It had been cleaned out and wood already laid, waiting to be used. A nice-looking couch and two recliners faced the fireplace with a table between the chairs and the couch. Destiny walked over to run her hand over the mantel and realized they'd finished it so it wasn't rough to the touch.

"The kitchen has a small gas stove that works until we run out of gas. Then we will have to install the cooking irons that allow you to swing pots over the fire," Marty said.

"I can cook over a fire. It's been a while, but Celina and I've been talking about it," she said.

"The refrigerator is clean and can be used for storage. There's a cold box buried next to the cabin so when it snows we can keep things cold out in it," Granger told her.

They watched her look around the kitchen area and then led her into the other room. It was the bedroom and was much larger than their room in the lodge. It also had an attached bathroom. She was thrilled with the overly large bed and dresser as well. The mattress was perfect, and she patted it on either side of her.

"Sit down with me."

"Abe and Russell already had the mattress. They got several to fix the other cabins, too," Marty told her as they set down on either side of her.

Marty dropped the pack on the floor. She wondered what he had in it. In fact, she wondered what they thought still needed doing that hadn't been done. The cabin looked ready for them to move in to her.

"Guys. The cabin looks ready to me. What else are you planning to do to it? All it needs now are supplies and us," she said.

"We're working on the outside to fill in all the holes and cracks so it will stay warm during the winter. Plus, we really wanted to get some more things moved in that you might need, like a table and chairs for the kitchen."

"Oh. I hadn't even noticed there wasn't anywhere to eat." She chuckled. "We have a bed. What more did we need?"

"Hmm," Marty said, rolling over on top of her. "That sounds like an invitation if I ever heard one."

"I suppose we should christen the bedroom while we're here. We can do the other rooms once we move in," Granger added.

Destiny giggled and wrapped her arms around Marty. He kissed her, slipping his tongue into her mouth to explore and tease. She moaned into his mouth as he kneaded her ass with his fingers.

"Gonna have to get her out of that coat before you can go any further, man." Granger's amused voice had her giggling into Marty's mouth.

"Who put all this crap on you in the first place?" Marty muttered.

She sat up once he'd gotten off of her, and the two men helped her out of the coat and then continued to undress her. Destiny managed to get them out of their coats and had made a good start on the buttons on their shirts when Granger picked her up and tossed her on the bed. She bounced and rolled over to kneel as they finished stripping in front of her. She loved how their bodies were so different. Where Marty was leaner than Granger, both men were muscular and mouthwatering to look at.

Destiny didn't even notice Granger's facial scar anymore. It was just a part of him. Neither did she notice the scar on Marty's back shoulder. What she did notice was how delicious their tight abdomens were and the impressive erections between their legs. She wanted them so much her hands were shaking.

When both men climbed onto the bed, she found herself sandwiched between them with Marty at her back and Granger in front of her. Both men kissed her shoulders and nibbled on her neck. They all three collapsed to the bed, and for a few minutes, she wasn't sure who touched what as the sensations of their mouths and hands became overwhelming for a bit. Then Marty pulled back and climbed between her legs, moving them apart as wide as he could get them.

He claimed her gaze and held it while he slowly lowered his head and licked her pussy. She closed her eyes and moaned in pleasure. He ran his tongue down the inside of her thigh, then licked over her folds again before moving to the other thigh. Back and forth, he tormented her with brief licks to her pussy lips before kissing or nipping at another part of her body.

"Marty. Please. Don't tease me." She was burning up with need already.

Granger chuckled and pinched both nipples with his fingers while he licked over her bottom lip. "Take it, baby. Take everything we give you."

She felt the zing of his pinches all the way to her clit. Her skin felt too tight as her arousal built higher and higher. They were going to kill her with the anticipation of whatever they had in store for her.

"Look at how rosy her skin gets when she's aroused, Marty." Granger's voice had taken on that deep, husky quality that never failed to set her blood on fire.

"She tastes like pure sin," Marty told him. "Give me your finger, honey."

She released the hold she'd had on Granger's hair and lowered her hand toward where Marty lay between her legs.

"Now run your fingers through that juicy pussy for me," Marty crooned.

She slipped her finger into her pussy and gathered her juices, slipping her finger across her clit in the process.

"No, you don't, you little minx." Marty grabbed her wrist and stopped her from rubbing her clit. "Now give Granger a taste of your sweet honey."

She lifted her fingers to Granger. He held her wrist and sucked her fingers clean of her juices, making an appreciative noise as he did. It thrummed down her spine, sending chills along her skin. When he let go of her wrist, she grabbed his head and pulled him down for a kiss. She could taste herself on his mouth but delved deeper with her tongue to taste him and his unique flavor.

When she pulled back to gasp as Marty thrust two fingers deep into her cunt as he sucked hard on her clit, Destiny felt her climax rushing toward her. Granger leaned over and sucked one breast as far into his mouth as he could manage. Her nipples were so sensitive now that she was pregnant, but they didn't know that. She gasped when he pulled and pinched the other one.

Then Marty grasped her clit with his teeth and flicked it over and over again with the tip of his tongue, sending electrical sparks through her bloodstream. She screamed as her climax roared over her like a tsunami. She reached out and grabbed Granger's head in an effort to ground herself. The sensations were too much. She thought she would fly apart if she didn't hold on to something.

When she slowly began to calm down, Marty set up on his knees and barked out orders she normally heard from Granger.

"I want you riding Granger, Destiny. Climb on his cock for me."

She looked at Granger then back at Marty. What was he going to do?

"You heard him, babe. Park that pretty pussy on my dick. I'm going to take you on a ride, darling." Granger laid back and reached up to steady her as she climbed over to straddle his hips.

"Easy, babe." Granger held his cock steady as she slowly sank her wet, swollen pussy over his thick stalk.

They both moaned as she slid down him until her pussy rested flush with his groin. She swore he reached her throat. He filled her completely. Granger rested his big hands at her hips, squeezing them lightly as she fought to breathe. He pumped up into her, lifting her slightly as he did. She rose up, then sank down, sliding along his shaft so that her cunt burned with so much sensation she thought she would implode at the pressure he was building inside of her.

Marty pressed his hand between her shoulders and pressed her down over Granger's chest. She turned her face so that one cheek rested over where his heart beat, steady and comforting. The big man under her wrapped his arms around her, anchoring her in place as Marty rubbed and massaged her hips and ass cheeks. It suddenly dawned on her that Marty was going to take her ass. Hope flared in her heart that he'd come to terms with his wants and needs.

"Shh, baby. Let him settle," Granger whispered in her ear as if he had read her thoughts.

She relaxed against him as her other lover continued to squeeze and release the cheeks of her butt. Then he let go, and she heard the sound of something rustling behind her. The next thing she felt was cold lube of some type dripping down the cleft between her buttocks. He smoothed it down until he rubbed it around her back hole. Then more lube dripped there, and he pressed his finger into her back entrance. It easily slipped inside as he pushed it deeper then pulled out again.

More of the greasy lube, and he added a second finger. It took a little more pressure to push this one past her tight resistant ring, but it popped through with little discomfort to her. He paused a second, and she pushed back against him so he'd know he wasn't hurting her. He chuckled and popped her butt before pumping the two fingers in and out of her back hole until he seemed satisfied she was okay.

"Man, you add any more lube and you're going to catch hell getting enough traction to even fuck her ass," Granger teased the other man.

"Shut up, Granger. I'm not going to risk hurting her," Marty argued.

"I'm good, Marty. Fuck me. I need you inside me, Marty." Destiny wanted him to know she needed him there, just like she needed Granger.

"You tell me if it's too much, honey. Promise you will."

"I will, Marty. Hurry. Please."

Marty settled his cock at her tiny rosette and pressed forward. She felt him slip some, but he didn't ease up as the spongy head of his dick slowly slid inside her ass. She moaned at the pressure but pushed her ass back to help. The crown of his penis slipped past the resistant ring, and he stopped once he'd made it halfway.

"Ah, hell! So fucking hot. You're burning me alive, D. You're strangling my cock." Marty's strained voice was music to her ears.

"Move, Marty! Fuck me!" she all but screamed.

He pulled back until just the crown rested inside, then he surged forward and buried his dick all the way inside so that his balls slapped against her pussy. When he pulled back the next time, Granger surged upward, bringing her down on his hard shaft. They seesawed in and out of her in tandem until she no longer knew who was inside and who was waiting their turn. The mirage of sensations overwhelmed her nervous system, and she had no way to tell the difference between pain and pleasure, ecstasy and mind-blowing bliss. Everything seemed so much more intense. Nerves in her ass were screaming, adding to the burning in her cunt and the tingling and tightness in her clit. Even her nipples had grown achy and almost painful with the need for something she couldn't put her finger on.

"Oh, darling, D. You feel so good. With Marty in your hot ass, I don't have enough room to fucking think, much less breathe. I'm never going to last like this, baby. It's too fucking good." Granger leaned up and sucked one nipple inside his mouth even as he pushed between their bodies to reach her clit.

The three of them surged around each other, giving and taking the pleasure, the joy, the others were offering. Destiny was helpless to control any of it. Not her pleasure, and definitely not theirs. Granger's finger pressed tightly at her clit slowly built her impending climax to the point she was almost afraid of it. Each press of his pelvis as he surged inside of her increased the pressure to her clit. With one last indrawn breath, Destiny came apart in their arms, screaming and bucking between them.

"Holy hell!" Marty yelled after her.

She missed whatever Granger might have said or even yelled as her ears began to ring and she lost a few seconds of consciousness. The roaring in her head seemed to lessen at last, and she felt Marty's teeth release her shoulder where he'd closed over her there. She winced as he pulled back and then out of her. Then she collapsed back on Granger and drifted as the two men cleaned her up and situated her between them on the bed.

It took her a while to be able to form coherent thoughts, and a little longer for her to actually be able to put those thoughts into words. She was lying across Granger's big body with Marty hugging her back, his face buried in the back of her neck.

"Hmmm. What's with the biting, Marty? Are you really a werewolf and you just haven't told me yet?" she asked, a teasing note to her voice.

"Sorry about that. I, um, didn't realize what I was doing at the time." His muffled explanation sounded perfect to her.

"Mmm, I like your love bites," she assured him. "What's all the stuff I saw behind the cabin? It looks like you've cleared everything off to the side of this room."

"We're planning to add on and wanted to get a head start before winter," Granger said, his voice rumbling in her ear. "We've already added a loft we haven't shown you yet since the stairs aren't done. Then there's going to be another room off to the side."

"That sounds perfect. We'll need it soon, too," she said.

"Yeah, well, we figured it would be good for storage at first. We won't be able to actually work on it much until after we get the garden put in this spring," Marty added.

Granger stiffened beneath her. "Why are we going to need the other room, Destiny?"

"Well, I figure I'm going to want to keep the baby in with us for the first few months, but after that, she'll need to be in her own room as she gets older." Destiny held her breath, wondering how they were going to take her news.

There was absolute silence for several long seconds. She thought she was going to have to say something when Marty rolled away from her and jumped off the bed.

"Oh, hell. Why didn't you tell us before we did that to you? I might have hurt the baby. Fuck! Granger. Were you as rough as it felt like you were?" He paced back and forth in front of the bed.

"Well, hell, Destiny. You got him stirred up again, babe." Granger's chest started shaking, and she realized he was laughing.

She pushed off of him and scowled down at the man. "Why are you blaming this on me, and why are you laughing?"

"Settle down, D..."

"And when in the hell did you and Marty start calling me D?" she demanded.

Granger started laughing harder, then threw up his hands in defense when she started slapping at him.

"Answer me you, you Neanderthal!"

"Marty, help, man! She's going to hurt herself," Granger called out between chuckles and grunts from her strikes.

Marty stopped pacing and hurried over to the bed to pull her gently off of Granger. "Easy, ladybug, or you're going to get hurt. You have to be careful now that you're having our baby."

"I'm not made of glass, guys." Destiny wanted to scream at them. If they tried to treat her this way her entire pregnancy, she'd go stark-raving mad.

"It's a good thing we're staying in the lodge this winter," Marty said. "I sure as hell wouldn't want you out here while you were pregnant until we have it completely insulated and the doors reinforced."

"There's nothing wrong with it now. We can go ahead and move out here as far as I'm concerned," she said with a sweet smile.

She knew they wouldn't do that, but she took a small measure of perverse pleasure in seeing Granger pale at the thought.

"Oh, hell no!" he bellowed. "We're not moving out here until it's as safe as we can make it. No way, no how." He shook his head and crossed his arms.

He looked hilarious sitting there like that with his chin lifted and his arms crossed, wearing nothing but his stubborn expression. She started giggling, and they both froze, panicked expressions poured over their faces.

"What's wrong?" Marty asked, easing closer to her.

"Nothing. I was just so worried you'd be angry with me for getting pregnant that seeing you both like this in daddy-bear protective mode is cute," she said.

"Daddy bear? What the hell is that?" Granger asked with a huff.

"Never mind. So you're both okay with us having a baby so soon?" she asked.

She gnawed at her lower lip as she watched their faces for any hint of their true feelings. Marty's face softened, and he smiled. Granger's features relaxed as much as she'd ever seen them.

"Honey, you're having our baby. We're more than okay with it. We're proud as that papa bear you said something about," Marty said.

"Never thought I'd ever have kids, baby. The idea of a little girl with your beautiful eyes and the way they sparkle when you're excited or mad makes me sigh deep inside. I can't believe it," the big man said.

"I figure I'm due about the middle of June, but I could be off some. I, uh, was never very regular or anything anyway." Destiny knew by the heat rushing to her face that she was blushing.

"Fuck, you could be even further than that along, babe. I don't remember you ever having your period," Granger said with a frown.

"Yeah, well, I spotted here and there, but that's about all I usually do when I have one. Can we change the subject?" she asked. Her face felt as if she was standing in front of a blow torch.

"You're so cute when you blush," Marty teased.

She slapped at his hands when he pulled her into his arms. It didn't bother him. He just grinned and kissed her.

"Don't be embarrassed about that, darling," Granger said as he climbed out of bed and pressed his hot body against her back. "It's just another part of you. We love all of you, D."

"Why do you keep calling me D? My aunt used to call me Dessie, but no one has ever called me just D before."

"It's short for Destiny and darling. If you don't like it, we'll stop," Marty told her, a serious look in his eyes.

"It's fine. I don't mind. I just couldn't figure out where it had come from all of a sudden," she said.

"Oh, we've been calling you that behind your back for a long time, babe," Granger said with a chuckle. "You know, 'D is driving me crazy with her nagging all the time.'"

She growled and tried to turn so she could hit Granger. Marty laughed and held her tight between them.

"Easy, honey. You know he's teasing. You've got to be careful with our baby inside you. No horsing around anymore," Marty admonished.

"I don't horse around." She frowned at him.

"We'd better get back before it gets too late. It's already growing dark out there." Granger backed away from her to start getting dressed.

Marty kissed her and grabbed her underwear from the floor. When he handed it to her, she smiled gently at him and pulled him back to her for another kiss.

"I love you, Marty. I love all of you."

"I love you, too, ladybug." He got on his knees and kissed her belly. "I love you, too, baby bug."

"Hey, Marty. While you're down there, you need to propose to her, too. Make it official and all," Granger said, standing in just his jeans next to her.

"Get your ass down here, too. You have to propose to her, too," the other man said with a smirk.

"She might say no to one of us, but if she says yes to you, that includes me." Granger's grin was engaging, but Destiny was having none of it.

She walked around behind him and kneed him in the back of his knees, making his legs fold. He didn't fall, but he did ease to the floor and look up at her with what could only have been adoration in his eyes. Destiny blinked back the tears in her eyes then waited for them to speak.

"You know we both love you, Destiny, with all of our hearts and souls. We will do anything to make you happy and keep you safe," Marty said.

"And the baby, too," Granger added, pushing on Marty.

Marty frowned at the other man. "I was getting to that."

"Well, hurry up already."

"We want to spend the rest of our lives proving to you how much you mean to us. Will you and baby bug be ours?" Marty asked.

"Forever," Granger added.

"I love you both so much. I'll always be yours. Both of yours." Destiny sank to her knees to hug them.

"You're our Destiny, baby. And we're yours." Granger wrapped his arms around them.

Destiny smiled in the huddle. She didn't know what the future held for the three of them, now four, but she knew she would never regret trusting them with her safety and her heart.

THE END

WWW.MARLAMONROE.COM

ABOUT THE AUTHOR

Marla Monroe has been writing professionally for about ten years now. Her first book with Siren was published in January of 2011. She loves to write and spends every spare minute either at the keyboard or reading another Siren author. She writes everything from sizzling-hot contemporary cowboys, to science fiction ménages with the occasional bad-ass biker thrown in for good measure.

Marla lives in the southern US and works full-time at a busy hospital. When not writing, she loves to travel, spend time with her cats, and read. She's always eager to try something new and especially enjoys the research for her books. She loves to hear from readers about what they are looking for next. You can reach Marla at themarlamonroe@yahoo.com or visit her website at www.marlamonroe.com.

For all titles by Marla Monroe, please visit
www.bookstrand.com/marla-monroe

Siren Publishing, Inc.
www.SirenPublishing.com

Lightning Source UK Ltd.
Milton Keynes UK
UKOW04f2136120514

231562UK00020B/846/P